THE TRAGEDY OF ORENTHAL

PRINCE OF BRENTWOOD

THE TRAGEDY *of* ORENTHAL
PRINCE OF BRENTWOOD

MICHAEL W. MONK

SMALL BATCH BOOKS
AMHERST, MASSACHUSETTS

Copyright © 2012, 2014 by Michael W. Monk

All rights reserved.
No part of this book may be copied,
transmitted, or reproduced without permission.
Printed in the United States of America
on SFI®-certified, acid-free paper.

Designed by Bhairavi Patel
Cover design by Carolyn Eckert

Quotations in the text are taken from
The Arden Shakespeare Complete Works, Third Series, 1998

ISBN 978-1-937650-36-0
Library of Congress Control Number: 2012948871

SMALL
BATCH
BOOKS

493 SOUTH PLEASANT STREET
AMHERST, MASSACHUSETTS 01002
413.230.3943
SMALLBATCHBOOKS.COM

For Janet, Susannah, and James,
who have supported and encouraged
my fondness for the Bard

PREFACE

In 1998 my family and I traveled to England. We were to stay one week in London and one week in Stratford. I had concentrated in English literature as an undergraduate, and my fondness for Shakespeare had only grown over the years. In anticipation of this trip, I began to reread Shakespeare's plays, probably a dozen or so before we arrived in Stratford. It was no surprise that the more I read the plays, the more accessible and clear they became. The rhythm and feel of the blank verse and iambic pentameter slowly became ingrained in my consciousness.

As I reread the tragedies of *Macbeth* and *Othello*, in particular, many of the passages seemed to echo what I imagined O.J. Simpson might have been thinking just before and just after the murders of Nicole and Ronald Goldman. It struck me that indeed Simpson was like a Shakespearean tragic hero, brought down from renown and fame by a fatal flaw—jealousy. I started to highlight passages in the plays that might apply to the Simpson story. Why not try to tell the whole Simpson story in the Shakespearean format, with blank verse, five acts, stage direction, etc.? The idea captivated me, in part because it would be a chance to have some fun with the blank verse format and to include modern vernacular with some of the Elizabethan language. Equally compelling was a chance to tell the Simpson story as I speculate it really happened.

In *The Tragedy of Orenthal, Prince of Brentwood* I have attempted to write a play telling the story of Orenthal J. Simpson in the style, verse, and format of William Shakespeare. The play contains approximately 2,600 lines of original verse. Incorporated into the original verse are thirty-seven separate quotes taken directly from

Shakespeare, where the language is particularly apt to the Simpson story. The thirty-seven quotes, comprising approximately 215 lines, are generally taken verbatim or virtually verbatim. Minor changes incorporate the names and circumstances of the Simpson story. Each quote is identified in the Notes section at the end of the play. The Notes section identifies the exact source of the quote, with references to the text of *The Arden Shakespeare Complete Works*, Third Series.

Orenthal is written mostly in blank verse and divided into five acts, with a prologue. The original blank verse contains a mixture of Elizabethan language and modern usage. The rhyming frequency is generally similar to Shakespearean blank verse; the slightly more frequent use of rhyme is typical of early comedies like *The Comedy of Errors* and *Love's Labour's Lost*.

The play's story is a blend of history and speculation. Many scenes are drawn from historical sources: Nicole Brown Simpson's 911 call, the note Simpson left when he fled arrest, the transcript of the telephone conversation during the slow-speed chase, the transcript of the police interview of Simpson, and court transcripts from the criminal trial. Background material was also drawn from *Evidence Dismissed* by detectives Tom Lange and Philip Vannatter (Pocket Books, a division of Simon & Schuster, copyright 1997) and *Outrage* by Vincent Bugliosi (W. W. Norton & Co., copyright 1996).

Other scenes are pure speculation: the murders of Nicole Brown Simpson and Ronald Goldman, Simpson's Maui golf game, Simpson's restaurant confrontation of Nicole and Goldman, the conversation between Kato Kaelin and Simpson on the trip to McDonald's the night of the murders, meetings between Simpson and his lawyers, and Simpson's soliloquies expressing his innermost thoughts. Even when events are drawn from news accounts—for example, the Rosey Grier visit to Simpson in jail—the language and speeches of the characters are generally fictional, composed to create a work of literature rather than an exact history.

THE TRAGEDY OF ORENTHAL

Whether this play is a tragedy, a tragicomedy, a parody, or a crypto-parody, I leave to the reader. The use of Shakespearean language and verse mixed with current language to address this modern story is often naturally amusing. I hope, however, as the play develops, this style will be seen not only to provide humor, but also to address serious themes and emotions.

MICHAEL W. MONK
March 2014
Santa Monica, California

ACKNOWLEDGMENTS

I want to take the time thank my publisher, Small Batch Books. Fred Levine and Trisha Thompson have been supportive and consistently wise in their editorial guidance, while simultaneously projecting the warmth and cordiality of a family business. Thanks also to Bhairavi Patel for her careful book design and Carolyn Eckert for a killer cover.

I also want to thank my friends and family who gave the book a close reading and offered advice in the drafting stage, including my wife Janet, my son James, my daughter Susannah, and my long-time friend, lawyer, and author, Jonathan Fraser Light. Their suggestions were invaluable. Many thanks also to my friend Henry Dearing, who has been an enthusiastic and consistent supporter of the project.

I also want to give credit to Henry's late father, Vinton Dearing, who passed away in 2005. Vinton Dearing was a UCLA professor and Dryden scholar, renowned in academic circles. He read my draft and generously advised me on the use of Elizabethan language mixed with modern vernacular.

—*M.W.M.*

INTRODUCTION

This year marks the twentieth anniversary of the murders of Nicole Brown Simpson and Ronald Goldman, on June 12, 1994. The murders and the subsequent trial of once-popular football star turned actor Orenthal James (O.J.) Simpson held the nation in suspense for months. On October 3, 1995, I stood in a law office conference room in Orange County, California, watching the small television and awaiting the jury's verdicts on the double murder. I was representing a client in a deposition that day but stopped what I was doing, along with everyone else at the law office, to watch with nervous anticipation as the court clerk haltingly announced Simpson as "not guilty" on all counts. Simpson mouthed "thank you" to the jury and hugged his attorneys.

Those who followed the trial closely will always remember that day and where they were when they learned of the verdict. I was stunned both at the verdict and the short time the jury took to reach its decision. The trial had lasted eleven months and involved what seemed like many pieces of evidence that could have independently confirmed Simpson as the murderer. Nevertheless, the jury deliberated for only four hours before returning the not-guilty verdict.

Later that evening, I saw a national news broadcast of students at the University of Indiana Law School in a lounge watching as the verdict was announced on television. The Caucasian students stared at the TV in silence. The African-American students cheered.

The law students' responses turned out to be a microcosm of the nation's responses. Some saw the O.J. verdict as making up for the recent decision to set free the white police officer who had beaten Rodney King, a demonstration that African Americans can get justice. Others saw a tragic miscarriage of justice and a complete failure of the jury system. Simpson's lawyer, Johnnie Cochran, had transformed the issue from whether O.J. Simpson had killed two people in cold blood to whether African Americans deserve justice.

Twenty years after the murders, many still have vivid memories of the trial scenes and the controversial verdict. But the trial was such a confused blending of advocacy, irrelevancy, race, and outrage, that many of the facts, as they stand alone, have faded. One of my reasons for writing this play was to summarize the history and its facts and make reasonable speculation about what likely happened behind the scenes. The play also examines the psychology of Simpson, in an effort to explain his actions. Another strong motivation for this work was the joy of playing with Shakespearean language. I had tremendous fun using the blank verse format to include current vernacular, slang, and even profanity, mixed with Elizabethan language, all filtered through the structure of iambic pentameter. The Simpson story seemed a perfect match for this linguistic format in that it possesses so many aspects of the classic Shakespearean tragedy, including the fatal flaw leading to the downfall of the protagonist.

The emotion and drama of this grisly but fascinating, and at times even comical, modern tragedy still resonate with us today. As 2014 marks the twentieth anniversary of the murders, I hope *The Tragedy of Orenthal* will help readers recall both what we know occurred and what we think may have occurred on the night of June 12, 1994.

—*M.W.M.*

THE TRAGEDY OF ORENTHAL

PRINCE OF BRENTWOOD

DRAMATIS PERSONAE

ORENTHAL   Orenthal J. Simpson, Prince of Brentwood.

NICOLE   Princess of Brentwood, Orenthal's ex-wife and mother to Sydney and Justin, Orenthal's two younger children.

RONALD GOLDMAN,   friends to Princess Nicole.
LADY GARVEY

SYDNEY, JUSTIN   children to Orenthal by Nicole.

ARNELLE, JASON   children to Orenthal by his first wife.

COWLINGS, KAELIN,   attendants to Orenthal.
KARDASHIAN

DENISE BROWN,   sisters to Nicole.
DOMINIQUE BROWN

LOU BROWN,   parents to Nicole.
JUDITHA BROWN

VANNATTER, LANGE, FUHRMAN, PHILLIPS, GASCON	constables.
COCHRAN, SHAPIRO, SCHECK, BAILEY	counselors to Orenthal.
CLARK, DARDEN, COURTIERS	counselors to the State of California.
JUDGE ITO	
FELIX	Olympic medalist and African American friend to Orenthal.
PARM, STORM	Caucasian law partners of Felix.
ROSEY GRIER	man of the cloth and friend to Orenthal.
JURORS AND COURT PERSONNEL	
PRINCE'S MOTHER	
COURT CLERK	
REPORTERS	
BELLHOP	

THE TRAGEDY OF ORENTHAL

DESK CLERK

PARENT OF FRIEND TO SYDNEY

MAÎTRE D'

RESTAURANT PATRONS

ATTENDANTS

GOLFERS

CHORUS

SCENE: *Brentwood and environs.*

PROLOGUE

Enter Chorus.

CHORUS.   I tell a tale of murder: Goldman and Nicole
          Are now dead; give order that their bodies
          High on a stage be placed to the view;
          And let me speak to the yet unknowing world
          How these things came about. So shall you hear
          Of carnal, bloody, and unnatural acts,
          Of accidental judgments, casual slaughters,
          Of deaths put on by cunning and forc'd cause,
          And, in this upshot, purposes mistook
          Fall'n on th'inventors' heads. All this can I
          Truly deliver.[1]

ACT I

SCENE 1
(The parking lot of the Los Angeles Forum, 1985)

Enter Orenthal and Nicole, leaving the parking lot in a Bentley, and Felix, Parm, and Storm, leaving the parking lot in a Mercedes sedan.

PARM. The Laker five doth run the floor with style,
Dispatching foe effectively this eve.
Straight down the court they race and sprint and leap,
Like gazelles graceful, bounding o'er the plain.
Relentless for each tip and high rebound,
They soar above opponents on the ground.

FELIX. They seem a team inspired to win 'gainst all,
Blessed by a Magic man who guides the way;
He lifts their spirits and their destiny,
With fire that burns and grace that doth amaze.

PARM. Showtime displayed 'fore minions large and loud,
With dancing girls to tantalize the crowd.
The faces fair and debonair abound,
Celebrities all surfeited with sound.

STORM. What ho? Who goes in yonder wheels of white?

PARM. Which one? The Bentley that's bereft of top?

STORM. The one with plate "L84AD8."

PARM. A handsome Moor behind the wheel, next to a beauty fair
With features fine of Nordic clime and silky golden hair.

FELIX. That's Orenthal! I pray pull to his side,
A friend of mine from college school days past.
We ran the sprint events at local schools,
A Bruin I, a Trojan proud was he,
Some years ago to glory sprinted we.

[To Orenthal.]
Say hey! Prince Juice! How goes the fray for thee?

ORENTHAL. Quite well, I do complain not of my state.
And you, Felix, of sweet Olympic fame?

FELIX. I, too, fare well, the truth to tell, a lawyer's cloth
I wear each day.

ORENTHAL. And dear Felix, how fares thy family?

FELIX. My sons grow tall, our lives proceed apace
In harmony my bride and I do dwell.

ORENTHAL. Adieu and God bless you,
Be true to thine own desires.

FELIX. Adieu, sweet Prince, and God guide you.

Exeunt Orenthal and Princess Nicole.

THE TRAGEDY OF ORENTHAL

PARM. Felix! She is indeed a Goddess true,
She robs my breath as she herself doth breathe.
A face with classic form and shape divine,
Dear God that such a creature 'ere were mine.

FELIX. Oh, she doth teach the torches to burn bright!
It seems she hangs upon the cheek of night
Like a rich jewel in an Ethiop's ear
Beauty too rich for use, for earth too dear![2]

STORM. Is she the love and bride of Juice himself?

FELIX. She is indeed his Princess and his wife,
A vision who illuminates his life.

STORM. So much success for just one human soul:
A football God of storied Heisman fame,
Electrifying runs for Trojan gain,
Still greater peaks he scaled in Buffalo,
Two thousand yards he was the first to know.
He rises to the heavens as the one,
But will he fly too closely to the sun?

PARM. Not so, I say, Prince Juice is on the rise,
A superstar for rent-a-car his guise.
A sideline man with microphone in hand,
He charms his movie fans across the land.
Beloved by races all, by rich and poor,
Though black as night, he's opened every door.

FELIX. While fetid bigots there will always be,
Acceptance hath most generally come for me.
And equally so for the flashy Juice.

The hallowed words of prescient Doctor King,
Hath to some small extent now come to be:
To judge a man not by his skin or hue,
But by his deeds and character so true.

Storm. Prince Juice sleeps in the bed of luxury
Estates, maids, Bentleys, private schools, fine wines,
Vacations, Learjets, bistros of a kind.

Felix. But think'st thou it's the wealth he prizes most?
Is adulation not as sweet a fruit?
Worshipped by the masses, what a rush!
He basketh in the sun of public love.

Storm. Your "sun of public love" is more a moon,
Since changeable, it waxes and it wanes.
Methinks more treasured are his worldly goods,
Like most who rose from modest ways and means.
The ones who discount wealth are mostly rich,
The poor respect the buck with no pretense.

Parm. His license plate reflects upon his state
"L84AD8"... "Late for a date."
The words of a dude who doteth on himself
With little care for those he doth delay.

Felix. No, I have found him more a gentle man,
With confidence and cordiality.
Let's drive!

Exeunt.

SCENE 2
(Maui golf course, 1990)

Enter Orenthal, Cowlings, and attendants; sound a flourish.

ORENTHAL. The verdant lawn doth smell so sweet this morn.
This Prince will spend the day in paradise.
Kahualawe looms upon my right,
Perched on the vast Pacific azure pond.
My clubs are striking well for all to see,
Drives, pitches, chips, and draws so nicely hit.
A more idyllic life will not ensue,
When this is all the work that I must do.

COWLINGS. I'm sure it shocks few people in the realm,
That thou liv'st with a modicum of bliss.

ORENTHAL. Thy jest doth strike the mark, I do admit.
A blessed Prince indeed is what I am.
To see me as a babe one would not guess
That lucrative engagement would be mine.
Most would have said a hustler on the street
Would be the fate this ghetto child would meet.
Yet here I stand celebrity and star,
With pretty friends who helped to take me far.
I'm doted on by all I see and meet,
Sweet fame for me remains a joyous treat.

COWLINGS. My Lord, your turn is up, prepare to hit.
The green now sits, awaiting your approach.

ORENTHAL.   Quite so, the hole is placed upon the right.
            I'll seek to fade the ball with all my might.
            What think'st thou? Should I seek a hole in one?
            Or with sweet maid one in the hole so tight?

ATTENDANTS. The whole of one is more than one can hole,
            If beauty fair doth shield what we extol.

ORENTHAL.   Of golf, the soul revolves around the hole
            From which a flag waves on a sturdy pole.
            In just one shot to stick it in the hole
            Will place the golfer on the honor roll.

ATTENDANTS. But beauty fair wants more than just one shot
            When lover's soft caresses make her hot.

COWLINGS.   Good Prince, do you intend to talk or hit?

ORENTHAL.   With patience you must let me take my hack,
            And give me space, my friend, well off my back.

ATTENDANTS. Quite so, your Lordship, we agree, your Grace,
            No need to speed the game to such a pace.

COWLINGS.   Come, come, Prince Juice, please hit while we are young.

Exeunt.

THE TRAGEDY OF ORENTHAL

SCENE 3
(*The clubhouse bar at the Maui golf course*)

Enter Orenthal and Cowlings to have a private drink.

COWLINGS. This scenic isle, it soothes my tired mind,
Provides a respite from the earthly grind.

ORENTHAL. For me it serves a time to contemplate,
To calmly judge my life, assess my state.
To ponder just what course I should pursue
In matters that do plague my vision true.
Thus do I muse when I am far from home,
In either modest flat or pleasure dome.
A sharper focus grows in distant land
On that which we see not when close at hand.

COWLINGS. What demons plague thy most idyllic life?
Thou seldom play'st the melancholy fife.

ORENTHAL. I'm blessed with much to love and celebrate;
To hit my woods and jest for friends of Hertz
Is work I do enjoy, and who would not?
But life's broad sweep brings sour notes to me
As any human on this twirling orb.
My Princess fair and I have had our bouts.

COWLINGS. The tensions I have seen from time to time.
What now disturbs domestic bliss and peace?

ORENTHAL. We hold a different vision of our life
And quarrels have exploded, angry spats,
A jealous mate, she marks my every step,

And cannot be brushed back or pushed aside.
Domestic virtues? Few she hath displayed.
A sloppy house hath often me dismayed.
If maid has gone, the mess will not be touched,
No dinner on the plate when I come home.
Moreover, stubborn temper makes me roam.
While my liaisons she should now expect,
To all the world she must give me respect.

COWLINGS.   What hast thou done to curb such petulance?

ORENTHAL.   I've demonstrated that it soon must cease
With words and stern approach to emphasize.
On rare occasion I have smitten her,
When temper hath enveloped full my mind.
The New Year's spat last year left jagged scars,
Suggesting little peace is in our stars,
A messy scene, with cops and kids in tears,
She can't forsake me after all these years.

Exeunt.

SCENE 4
(Brentwood home of Princess Nicole, Monday, October 25, 1993)

Enter Nicole and Orenthal, now divorced.

NICOLE.   Will'st never my transgression thou forgive?
Small deed done in an age gone long ago!
Wouldst thou destroy the sanctity of dreams
Of our children now sleeping in their beds,

THE TRAGEDY OF ORENTHAL

          And terrorize your very flesh and blood?
          A coked-up bully, not a real man,
          You smash the very door to my abode.
          So, if you would, please kindly leave our state
          Of budding harmony and family ties.
          Piss off! Please haul your sorry ass away!
          You'll never sleep with me another day!
          Without Prince Scum I'll build a separate life;
          I'll ride the wave of freedom, free from fear.
          I will see who I want and when I will,
          I doubt, to stop me, you will deign to kill.
          Since we no longer live as man and wife,
          What purpose in reviving ancient strife?

ORENTHAL. Thy sordid acts splash shame upon my name:
          Thy open liaisons with pretty boys
          Who drive thy very car with mine own plate,
          And flaunt the way they plumb your every
             depth.
          Is it not I who funds each move you make,
          And underwrites your boys who mock my name?
          This is the home in which my children grow,
          That's now befouled by thee, thou little ho.
          You and your Resnick friend see dudes I doubt.
          The smell of sex and drugs surrounds you now,
          With shady "boyfriends" drifting in and out,
          You taint my children's sacred domicile
          As if in a bordello they did dwell.
          Indeed I do not need another source,
          Mine own eyes saw you locked in intercourse.

NICOLE.   Pathetic Peeping Tom thou hath become!
          Our prior life no license grants for these

Invasions rude that fright the little pair
Who issued from my loins, as you recall!
One half the blood that courses through
   their veins
Is mine and thus for them I would do all.
Insinuation that I would do less
Demeans me and insults my motherhood.
You own not them! You own not me! You fool.
Moreover, the example thou provid'st
Hath not been pure for Justin and Sydney.
You strayed with women when we still were wed
And took a goodly many to your bed.

Enter Kaelin, who observes the dispute.

NICOLE. Is this the tonic for our little ones?
They clearly see and sense all that you do.
While proof I've none, the rumors run
Of antics thou hast tried,
Though 'midst friends all, in parties small,
The stories will survive.
To point the blame at me you miss
The truth as well as your own bliss.

Nicole telephones 911.

[To the 911 operator.]
Please send the cops to Gretna Green forthwith,
A man broke down the door unto my house,
Prince Orenthal! He rants and screams and
   raves!
He's going to beat the life's breath out of me,
Please direct your resources with dispatch.

THE TRAGEDY OF ORENTHAL

                A friend who shares our home hath now arrived.
                He speaks with quiet calm now to the Prince.

KAELIN.   I pray, dear Prince, let's seek a quiet peace,
                We do not need a constable's firm hand.
                Emotions swell the pride and flame the mind,
                By shouts and screams such matters are not smoothed,
                But rather, please, at quiet place and time
                Address, resolve, and compromise benign.

ORENTHAL.   Tell me not how to fare with my ex-wife,
                Else I will light the night with flying fists.
                'Tis bad enough you live on her largesse,
                Residing upon the grounds of her estate.

KAELIN.   Forbear, know you too well I do no harm,
                I would not dare to advise you or her,
                I merely counsel peace for one and all.

ORENTHAL.   Your words contain the resonance of truth,
                But sorely miss the pain within my heart.

                [To Nicole.]
                And you, Nicole, don't condescend to me.
                Though proof I've none, the rumors run
                That Marcus thou hast laid.
                Wher' true or not, it leaves a spot,
                My reputation's frayed.

NICOLE.   Just go, please go, or cops will jail your ass.
                Bang not your fist upon my kitchen door.
                For one more E.R. trip I do not seek,

> As when you beat me with your "loving" hands,
> We lied to all the X-ray personnel
> And did pretend I tumbled from my bike.

ORENTHAL. Enough—I'm away! This is madness!

Orenthal walks alone to his car.

> My fury spent, foul demons drag me down.
> Too late for me a new life now to build.
> Rapacious harpies gnaw upon my soul.
> She seeks to cleanse herself from me, forsooth.
> I think of moments tender, intimate,
> With bodies linked in loving soft embrace.
> She used to soothe me with a whisper then,
> Like blue Pacific laps against the shore.
> Her lovely cheek I slowly would caress.
> I cannot be a stranger to Nicole.
> The mother of my children evermore,
> To share their lives and deeds, she holds the door.
> Do memories and passions past mean naught?
> Perhaps I should proceed and not look back.
> But when I look on her perfections,
> There is no reason but I shall be blind.
> If I can check my erring love, I will;
> If not, to compass her I'll use my skill.[3]

Exit.

THE TRAGEDY OF ORENTHAL

SCENE 5

(A restaurant in Brentwood, 1993)

Enter Orenthal, who approaches a table where Nicole is lunching with Goldman.

ORENTHAL. The air doth smell most foul at this repast.
It reeks of gutter rat and gigolo,
My Princess with a filthy spineless cur.

NICOLE. Thou hast no right to burst upon us now,
Like slinking panther dark thou stalk'st me.
I seek a moment's respite from your glare,
Do not an ugly scene make just for sport.
Your putrid presence no one here now needs,
I'll call security if this proceeds.

GOLDMAN. Nicole, I'll handle this without the law.
Prince Juice, we want no trouble here forsooth.
Nicole hath right to dine with whom she
    please.
With wisdom now withdraw and fade away.
Thy rude assault a loved one doth forsake,
You're better off your exit soon to take.

ORENTHAL. 'Tis best thou keep thy hands off her, my friend!
I've seen you cruising in my ragtop white,
As if thou ownest it, which thou dost not.
Recall that I did purchase those sweet wheels,
And trust that I invested not for thee
To peel around Brentwood with hairy chest,
You're but a doting slimy sycophant.

21

NICOLE. Remove your face from that of my male guest!
Remember who thou art and what thou dost!
I will not be intimidated from
Enjoying any man that I desire.

ORENTHAL. A trashy whore is all that you've become.
Your reputation shades both thee and me.
For Justin and for Sydney please relent.
We are forever bound together tight,
I'm with you always, deep into the night.

NICOLE. We are divorced! We are no longer wed!
Dost thou not see thou dost not rule my flesh!
Thou can'st not stop me by any earthly means.

ORENTHAL. Heed not her words, my friend, but list' to mine:
Thou'd best be far from her, I tell thee true.
I will not tolerate such insolence,
To keep thy teeth intact, thou best butt out!

NICOLE. Thou provokest public scene of most distaste.

ORENTHAL. It's little measured by what I would do
To ease the pain that I endure from thee.
Not idle jest nor isolated spat,
Trust me, that I will take this to the mat.

Enter maître d' of restaurant.

MAÎTRE D'. Good Prince, your pardon I do humbly beg,
Appropriate respect I do extend.
But I must ask thee now to come outside;
This isn't best the time, or best the place,

THE TRAGEDY OF ORENTHAL

                For matters thus so grave and personal.
                I'd like for you to walk with me forthwith.
                A Prince of highest eminence and fame,
                Thy spirit I do not wish to inflame.

ORENTHAL.   I will forbear! You've nothing here to fear.
                Much better things I clearly will pursue,
                So stand aside, and I will soon depart.
                If valet park can now retrieve my car,
                Your precious peace no longer will I mar.

MAÎTRE D'.   Your vehicle's return I will command,
                I thank thee humbly for thy helping hand.

                Exeunt Orenthal and maître d'.

NICOLE.   His rage and jealousy are nothing new,
                His fiery fits, a million I've endured.
                A different beast he is when on the prowl.
                I fear I can't escape his mission foul.

GOLDMAN.   Perhaps enjoin him with a legal suit
                Pursued posthaste in local civil court?
                I know such orders are obtainable
                To regulate a stalking former spouse.

NICOLE.   His fame and notoriety are known
                To judges and the constables of town.
                You can't restrain an icon like the Prince,
                Or think a court can regulate a man.
                It would just more excite his mental state;
                I fear that better times I must await.

SCENE 6

(Brentwood Country Club, Monday, January 17, 1994, at 10:37 a.m., six hours after the Northridge earthquake)

Enter Felix, Parm, and Storm.

FELIX. The night has been unruly: where we lay,
Our chimneys were blown down; and, as they say,
Lamentings heard i'th'air; strange screams of death;
And prophesying, with accents terrible,
Of dire combustion and confused events
New hatcht to th'woeful time: the obscure bird
Clamour'd the livelong night: and then the earth
Was feverous and did shake.[4]

STORM. Poor baby, didst the shaking frighten thee?
I'll fetch a pacifier you can suck.

PARM. The shaking woke me in the early day,
I think it was 4:30, ere daylight.
My house swayed back and forth disturbingly,
Books, dishes, art, and crystal all did fall
Down crashing on the floor in symphony.
I felt as in a ship tossed on the sea,
Pitching to and fro, 'midst swells and foam,
With gnarly Neptune blowing merrily.

STORM. The rides at Disneyland cause me more fright,
I slept just like an infant through the night.

FELIX. To me it was a most unsettling morn
That doth portend of evil still to come.

THE TRAGEDY OF ORENTHAL

                Why hath it happed upon a holiday,
                The birth of Martin Luther King to mark?
                The racial riots of the year just passed
                Methinks have not yet settled to a peace.
                Doth Zeus with thunderbolt seek to remind
                To heed only humanity, not hue?
                Or do the Gods rebuke hypocrisy
                Of charlatans manipulating race?

PARM.   What e'er may be the cause or origin,
                Thou seest the heavens, as troubled with man's act,
                Threatens his bloody stage.[5]

STORM.   In total fantasy you both engage,
                If serious you are of such portents.
                Diseased nature oftentimes breaks forth
                In strange eruptions; oft the teeming earth
                Is with a kind of colic pinch'd and vex'd
                By the imprisoning of unruly wind
                Within her womb; which, for enlargement striving,
                Shakes the old beldam earth, and topples down
                Steeples and moss-grown towers.[6]
                The earth would still have shaken us awake
                If Mother's Day had been the holiday.

PARM.   Methinks there are diverse realities:
                One man's truth is another's fantasy.
                One man's trash is another man's treasure,
                One man's work is another man's leisure,
                One man's ceiling is another man's floor,
                One man's princess is another man's whore.

STORM.   Your Neptune, Zeus, Diana are a crock,
         In such mythology I place no stock.
         As for the Lord, our God, I do confess,
         That I cannot his meanings always guess.

PARM.   Is not the God Christ preached of on the Mount
         As much a myth as those you do discount?

FELIX.   Your musings theological I hope
         Are worthy of a bishop or a pope.
         I care not to dissect such cosmic wrath,
         Just let the Gods of golfing guide my path!

         Exeunt.

SCENE 7
(Paul Revere Junior High School, Pacific Palisades, California, Sunday, June 12, 1994, late afternoon)

Enter Orenthal, Nicole, sisters to Nicole, Lou Brown, Juditha Brown, Lady Garvey, parents of other performing children, and other attendees at school dance reception.

PARENT. Fast friends with your sweet Sydney is my girl.
         To meet you is a pleasure trip, sweet Prince.
         From Trojan days, I followed your success,
         And thank thee lustily for all thy deeds,
         You made the Trojan horse break quite a sweat
         And gave me memories I still hold fast.

THE TRAGEDY OF ORENTHAL

ORENTHAL.   Good Sir, I thank you for your words so kind.
　　　　　　Those days mean much to me I must admit,
　　　　　　I never tire of telling Trojan tales,
　　　　　　Some sunshine thou hath brought into my day.
　　　　　　The memories blossom like a fragrant rose
　　　　　　When pigskin moments I do recollect.
　　　　　　The best I wish to you! Your daughter, too!

PARENT.   Godspeed and fare thee well!

ORENTHAL.   Be true to thine own desires!

　　　　　　[Aside.]
　　　　　　Play not the role of angered spouse,
　　　　　　But charming, smile to all the house.
　　　　　　This litany my actions guide,
　　　　　　I'll mask my feelings well inside.

　　　　　　Enter Nicole, Lady Garvey, and attendants.

NICOLE.   Oh joy, Prince Juice hath joined us here today.
　　　　　　I loathe to see him mingle, strut, and smile.
　　　　　　Where is that Barbieri girl he sees?
　　　　　　Wherefore is she not draped upon his arm?
　　　　　　For me to just ignore him is the best.

LADY   Dear Prince, what think'st thou of Sydney's
GARVEY.   　　dance?

ORENTHAL.   Her nimble steps produce parental pride,
　　　　　　Unmitigated rapture I confide.

LADY GARVEY.	Prince Orenthal, on that our minds are one. But seem you most distracted, what's the rub?
ORENTHAL.	'Tis nothing, I am fine and well, you see. A parent of this lass I'm proud to be.

Exit Orenthal.

NICOLE.	*[To Lady Garvey.]* Hello, dear friend, how farest thou today? At Mezzaluna we will dine this eve, With sisters, parents, Justin, Sydney, too. Prince Juice, he will not join us at this fest. Since our decision late to separate, 'Twould only mislead all and more confuse Our children, who must know that we are split.
LADY GARVEY.	'Tis now a fortnight since you called it off, Determined reconciliation failed. Doth he remain unsure about such course?
NICOLE.	He cannot leave us be, to have our peace. He best look forward and forget the past. I've told him nevermore will we to bed; The passion once I felt is clearly dead. And so tonight with family I dine, He can pursue whatever he may find. My wisdom comes, I know, a little late, But here I am, by history and fate.

Enter Orenthal, musing by himself.

THE TRAGEDY OF ORENTHAL

ORENTHAL.   [Aside.]
             Petulant shrew and marital sinner,
             She keeps me from my children's dinner?
             These precious windows to my children's youth
             Cannot be e'er regained in future days,
             But fade away so quickly and are gone.
             My face, in truth, is a book, where men
             May read strange matters. To beguile the time,
             Look like the time; bear welcome in your eye
             Your hand, your tongue: look like the
                innocent flower,
             But be the serpent under't. She that's coming
             Must be provided for; and I shall put
             This night's great business into my dispatch.[7]

LOU BROWN.   Hello, Prince Orenthal, how farest thou?

ORENTHAL.   My daughter lifts my spirits to the sky.
             By measures all, she is the rarest jewel.
             Now whither thee and the good Mrs. Brown?

JUDITHA   We plan to rendezvous at restaurant
BROWN.   To toast our Sydney 'midst the family.
             Fare thee well!

             Exeunt all but Orenthal.

ORENTHAL.   Ah, Mrs. Brown, you've got a lovely daughter.
             Would only she were once again mine own.
             I fare quite well with parents of Nicole.
             Oh, would that she would treat me as they do.
             Her condescending tone I cannot brook,
             She tenders me affront and surly look.

29

Just who is she to slice me with insult,
And humble me, withholding my offspring?
My flesh and blood I will not yield to her!
But reason does not penetrate her skull;
To no avail is charm or courtesy.
Her loveliness I can no longer taste;
She is to me but warden to my babes.
I watch her flirt with random trashy fools,
And constantly besmirch my name and life.
She boasts of newfound freedom and resolve
To shield each little private move from me
And forge a fearsome exclusivity.

Orenthal enters his car and drives home.

ORENTHAL. Oh temptress vile, I'll take her by the throat,
And from her pretty body, life I'll squeeze!
This strumpet will not longer toy with me,
But I will take control of destiny!
If she such pain continues me to give,
What benefit for her to longer live?

Exit.

ACT II

SCENE 1

(Prince Orenthal's estate in Brentwood, Sunday, June 12, 1994, at 9:10 p.m.)

Enter Orenthal.

ORENTHAL.   Chicago bags and golf clubs I have packed.
My Bronco's full of necessary gear:
Long-handled shovel, Bronco's plastic bag,
From which the tire and jack I have removed.
In sports bag small and black I always keep
A towel, gloves, tees and balls, a dark knit cap,
Sunglasses, golf cleats, hats, and my new knife.
I've also placed an extra set of clothes,
To camouflage my body all in black.
As if eternal lurking criminal,
I plot and contemplate my sweet revenge.
I must proceed if all the stars align
And I can lure her out into the yard;
Such business cannot wake a sleeping child.
Who e'er would guess such foul activity
Would so obsess a superstar like me.
This little witch I cannot let run free
To soil my name and bring me misery.
If fated night creates a chance that's gold,
I may effect my murder mission bold.
I must wait for the moment of a life
Before I teach her lessons with my knife
My fury at Nicole I cannot still,
It dominates my life and stirs my will!

Orenthal walks to the guesthouse used by Kato Kaelin.

But first I need an alibi so tight,
By spending time with Kato on this night.
He'll join me in whatever I propose,
A squatter has so little leverage.

Orenthal knocks at door of guesthouse. Enter Kaelin, who opens the door.

KAELIN. How now? Who's he that pounds upon my door?

ORENTHAL. Good Kato, if it pleases thee, 'tis I.
One moment of your time I do implore.

KAELIN. Of course, Prince Juice! By all means please come in!
How fares our Prince this eve?

ORENTHAL. A red-eye flight tonight is next for me,
I seek the windy city on the lake,
For golfing gig with dignitaries Hertz.
But currency, in small bills, I have none.
No skycap tip, a hundred dollar bill,
I need a ten or twenty, if you will?

KAELIN. I'll see, Prince Juice, what bills I do possess,
My pleasure to assist your every need.
Yes, here's a twenty dollar note for thee.

ORENTHAL. I'm off to find a fast food meal,

THE TRAGEDY OF ORENTHAL

	I've naught but little time, Dost thou feel like McDonald's fare? It's certainly no crime.
KAELIN.	Forsooth, I crave McDonald's much as thou, Perhaps a pleasing Happy Meal for me, A princely road trip suits me well, you see!
ORENTHAL.	Then join me in the Bentley, sans delay.
	Orenthal and Kaelin climb in the Bentley, and Orenthal begins to drive.
KAELIN.	What route dost thou pursue to seek the Duck?
ORENTHAL.	First Ashford down to Bristol, take a right, Next south on Bristol right across Sunset, South still to San Vicente Boulevard, A right to 26th and then a left, Then south to Santa Monica you go, At which a left will find the Golden Arch.
KAELIN.	A most sagacious path, I do concur.
ORENTHAL.	Fatigued am I, my day began at five, First golfing, cards, then to recital dance. Then pack for red-eye flight I take tonight. So weary, I may try to take a nap.
KAELIN.	Did Paula join thee for dear Sydney's dance?
ORENTHAL.	She did not, though she begged to come with me, But more a family time I had in mind,

So I refused, did not vouchsafe her wish,
She wanted all to see that I'm her man,
And strut beside me 'midst my family.
Her absence, though, produced not harmony.
I could not join the family dinner group,
And saw I little of my daughter dear.
All in all, Nicole looked like a fool.
She and her cronies wore their skirts so tight,
More like a strumpet bold, than mother fair.
As grandmothers I wonder what they'll wear.

KAELIN. They cling to youth as the mountain climber clings
Unto the steepest rocky precipice.
To lose their grip on youth would kill them, too.
Their short skirts will survive,
So long as bodies do.

ORENTHAL. Nicole and I are cruelly cleft in twain.
She's gone. I am abused, and my relief
Must be to loathe her. Oh, curse of marriage,
That we can call these delicate creatures ours,
And not their appetites! I had rather be a toad
And live upon the vapor of a dungeon
Than keep a corner in the thing I love
For others' uses. Yet 'tis the plague to great ones;
Prerogatived are they less than the base.
'Tis destiny unshunnable, like death.
Even then this fork'd plague is fated to us
When we do quicken.[8]

KAELIN. These sorrows will abate as weeks proceed,
To act in haste there clearly is no need.

THE TRAGEDY OF ORENTHAL

                  Good fortune swirls around thy very orb.
                  This wee bump in the road thou can'st absorb.

ORENTHAL.   Thy sanguine view, I fear, is quite naive.

KAELIN.   The Arch approaches fast upon the right.

ORENTHAL.   We're here, what meal for thee to take away?

KAELIN.   Large fries, a burger, and a Coke for me,
                  Not the white powder, but the drink, you see.

ORENTHAL.   Good takeout clerk, how now with thee this eve?
                  No complicated order will I weave.
                  Just doubles on the burgers, fries, and Cokes,
                  No nuggets, shakes, or apple pie to go.

KAELIN.   The greasy smell alone doth tease my buds,
                  No matter that it tends to clog the heart.

ORENTHAL.   My heart's in such turmoil that I care not.
                  As I am famished, I eat whilst I drive.
                  Here is your food and I will keep the change.
                  I'll add it to my skycap fund forthwith.

KAELIN.   With great dispatch you hurdle through the night,
                  Beware the Ford Explorer on the right!

ORENTHAL.   Relax thy soul, I know full what I do,
                  I'll drive thee safely home without ado.
                  Reflexes Heisman I do still possess,
                  How could'st thou ever suspect any less?

KAELIN. With confidence, I'll be a silent guest.

The Bentley arrives at Prince Orenthal's estate.

ORENTHAL. Adieu, Kato, I bid thee now farewell.

KAELIN. Farewell!

[Aside.]
I'll eat alone in my bungalow.

Exit Kaelin.

ORENTHAL. I must become a borrower of the night.
For a dark hour, or twain.[9]
Dark clothes to suit the dark revenge I seek
And knitted cap just like a common thief.
I've barely time before my airplane flies
To take the steps to make this matter right:
Strong measures that will rectify my plight.

Exit.

THE TRAGEDY OF ORENTHAL

SCENE 2
(Prince Orenthal's Bronco, Sunday, June 12, 1994, at about 9:50 p.m.)

Enter Prince Orenthal driving to Princess Nicole's Bundy condominium.

ORENTHAL. My cellphone call to Paula doth suggest
That flighty Barbieri hath left town.
Our fledgling romance hath begun to crack,
And reconstruction now may be too late.
These brazen women plague my every step!
If fated cards no aces hold for me,
I can cause unexpected misery.
Might I, someday, enjoy my children's lives?
Or will imprisoned they forever be?
Methinks she'd not forever shut me out.
But yet I'll make assurance double sure.
And take a bond of Fate: she shalt not live;
That I may tell pale-hearted fear it lies,
And sleep in spite of thunder.[10]
Present fears
Are less than horrible imaginings,
My thought, whose murder yet is but
  fantastical,
Shakes so my single state of man,
That function is smother'd in surmise
And nothing is, but what is not.[11]
Stars, hide your fires!
Let not light see my black and deep desires;
The eye wink at the hand; yet let that be,
Which the eye fears, when it is done, to see.[12]

37

SCENE 3

(Princess Nicole's Bundy condominium)

Enter Orenthal, who parks the Bronco in the alley behind Princess Nicole's condo.

ORENTHAL. The Bronco dome light I have now unscrewed
So darkness shan't be broken by its rays.
My blade I now have quietly secured,
I must confront the devil in my life.
If chance be there tonight, I do not know,
But soon she'll taste the wrath I will bestow.
And so I do implore thee! Come, thick Night,
And pall thee in the dunnest smoke of Hell,
That my keen knife see not the wound it makes,
Nor heaven peep through the blanket of the dark,
To cry, "Hold, hold!"[13]
I'll creep round to the front and buzz the gate,
And since the mechanism is impaired,
The gate she cannot open from inside.
She must forthwith proceed to meet the door.
I knock upon the gate with lightest touch.

Enter Nicole.

NICOLE. By the pricking of my thumbs,
Something wicked this way comes.
Open, locks,
Whoever knocks.[14]
Get thee away and not to nunnery,
But to cuckolded husband company.
You loathed, foul, impotent cockbite,
Go fuck yourself again and not too tight.

THE TRAGEDY OF ORENTHAL

ORENTHAL. No, fuck this knife, you slimy bitch!
Yes, fuck this knife in your soft throat!
That's right, this knife could slash your pretty neck,
And teach to you the lesson you must learn,
A simple schooling, just of loyalty,
And not, rude harlot, promiscuity.
Yes, fuck this knife and feel it penetrate,
And know that me thou no more will'st defy.

NICOLE. Oh, banish me, my lord, but kill me not.

ORENTHAL. Down, strumpet!

NICOLE. Kill me tomorrow; let me live tonight!

ORENTHAL. Nay, if you strive—

NICOLE. But half an hour!

ORENTHAL. Being done, there is no pause—

NICOLE. But while I say one prayer!

ORENTHAL. It is too late.[15]

Orenthal attacks Nicole, stabs her, and knocks her unconscious. Enter Goldman, who approaches from the front gate and enters the courtyard.

GOLDMAN. Stand ho! Who goes there?
What quarrel breaks the quiet of the night?
Nay, answer me: stand and unfold yourself!
Long live Princess Nicole![16]

Goldman sees Nicole twitching on the ground, Orenthal standing next to her.

God's grace, dark Prince, what nightmare
hast thou wrought!
What hath thy haughty temper done to Nic?
The very mother of your children dear!
You vile grotesque beast!

ORENTHAL. Come speak with me, thou faggot pretty boy.

GOLDMAN. Hey! Hey! Hey!

Orenthal leaps at Goldman and stabs him with the knife. In their grappling, Orenthal's knitted cap and left glove come off. Orenthal slices Goldman's palms as Goldman tries to defend himself; Orenthal cuts his own left middle finger. Finally, Goldman goes down.

GOLDMAN. Oh, serpent writhing 'midst your hellish mess,
Oh, such a putrid smell you do exude.
The world will know full well the deed you've
  done.
This day will haunt each moment of your life!

ORENTHAL. Your sniveling I will silence with my knife.

Orenthal cuts Goldman's throat from behind. Goldman dies. Princess Nicole begins to stir and moan.

NICOLE. Oh, monster that thou art! What hast thou done?
My breath will soon expire, extinguishing

THE TRAGEDY OF ORENTHAL

> My life and all its dreams for all the years.
> The constant fear becomes reality,
> I die!

ORENTHAL. You had your choice, and this is what you chose.

Orenthal puts his foot on her back, pulls Nicole's hair back, and slices her throat with the knife. Orenthal drops her lifeless corpse to the ground. Nicole's dog begins to bark.

> Oh! I have killed the woman who I love!
> What thin membrane lies twixt the quick and dead.
> One moment my sweet Helen's heart doth pound,
> Then she lay still, to breathe no nevermore,
> A prostrate butchered vision evermore.
> It is concluded: Nicole, thy soul's flight,
> If it find Heaven, must find it out tonight.[17]
> Dear Lord, I've slain them both.
> But witness to this deed I cannot brook.
> My soul is chilled with images of death,
> But single-minded now I must become,
> Cannot be paralyzed by shock or fear,
> Steadfast, dispose of evidence with care,
> And cleanse myself of trace to this red mess.
> I shall employ the focus and the skill
> Of concentration that I do possess,
> And tend to detail most meticulous.
> Like Mercury, I need to fly away,
> That I might live free for another day.

Nicole's dog, Kato, continues to bark at Orenthal and the slain bodies. Orenthal walks to the back gate toward the Bronco, then turns and returns toward the dead bodies.

But soft, I've lost my cap and my left glove
Removed 'midst the struggle and the death.
I must retrieve the bloody evidence.
But hark! I cannot!
The dog will quickly draw a crowd,
Even now I hear a passerby.
I cannot let another see me here,
And time to me is now becoming dear.

Orenthal enters the Bronco and drives away.

With haste this Bronco will speed me away
To a place I know of quiet privacy.
In alley's sanctuary none will hear,
Methodically I will arrange my gear.
As it's 10:32, I just have time
In my two bags to place my bloody things.
Dispose of all the traces to the scene,
Then power home to catch my limousine.

Exit.

THE TRAGEDY OF ORENTHAL

SCENE 4
(A secluded alley in Brentwood)

Enter Orenthal, who parks the Bronco.

ORENTHAL. Methodically each item I'll vouchsafe:
First soiled shoes I carefully will stow,
Next sweater, pants, and shirt I put aside.
With towel, hands and body I now wipe.
Then murderous knife in towel I will wrap,
Then clothing in the plastic bag I'll shove.
In my black bag I'll put the bloody glove.
The plastic bag in trash I will push down;
They cannot search each garbage can in town.
Next from my Bronco, extra clothing clean:
A shirt, my khaki pants, a pair of shoes.
Methinks that I have cleansed myself of blood.
There now, I'm no thug at a murder scene,
But just a local motorist it seems,
Though gruesome was the carnage left behind.
I must the ghastly images submerge,
Or in a pool of madness I may drown.
I have no time to feel emotions now.
Haste, haste! To home and then to plane away!
Reflection can occur another day.

Exit Orenthal in the Bronco, driving to his estate.

This enterprise hath even now been flawed,
Since Goldman ripped my left glove from my hand.
The pretty boy surprised me with his grip,
Mandating my wild slashes, to quiet him,

43

Augmenting much the bloody spectacle.
And my dark stocking cap I lost as well.
But never mind, I had no chance to search,
If I miss my plane, I'm in the lurch.
The cap and glove look like a million more,
If found they can't be placed upon my door.
No names or cute initials did they bear,
Just commonplace generic articles.
That which I can't control, I ponder not,
But focus on the things I can impact.
While entering the Bronco, I observed
Some bloody smears, but I did wipe them clean;
In any case, I'll soon be far from here.
So smooth and clean a mission I could see,
Had Goldman not a hero tried to be.

Exit.

SCENE 5
(Prince Orenthal's Rockingham estate)

Enter Orenthal, parking his Bronco askew outside his estate.

ORENTHAL. Alas, my limousine's already here,
I fear that its arrival is too quick,
Unlike my Princess, who is now quite dead.
I've little sensed the passage of the time.
Events have tumbled forth; come what, come may,
Time and the hour runs through the roughest day.[18]

THE TRAGEDY OF ORENTHAL

Straight through the front gate I cannot sashay,
But must appear to come from my estate,
The wall behind the bungalow I'll scale,
And enter soft as June's light zephyr blows.

Orenthal climbs noisily over the wall near Kaelin's guesthouse, with the second bloody glove falling out of the black sports bag. Orenthal then places the black bag in the driveway and enters his estate.

Will all great Neptune's ocean wash this blood
Clean from my hand? No, this my hand will
  rather
The multitudinous seas incarnadine,
Making the green one red.[19]
Some drops of blood still flow from my own flesh;
My middle finger has been sorely sliced,
A wound I suffered 'midst the recent fray
Close after my left glove fell to the grass.
God knows just where my dripping blood did fall.
The sissy boy created such a fuss.
Just what the hell brought him unto her house?
His little trip produced his just reward,
But now to more immediate concerns:
I'm clean and ready to proceed downstairs,
Where I must lightly grab my luggage black.
It hath surprises that must now be trashed,
Or prison will my next address soon be.
I must with bags to limousine proceed.
I see the driver waits for me,
I'm late for a date with destiny.

Exit.

SCENE 6
(Chicago Airport, O'Hare Plaza Hotel, Monday, June 13, 1994, at 5:30 a.m.)

Enter Orenthal, emerging from taxi in front of hotel, bellhop, and desk clerk.

BELLHOP. My warmest welcome I extend to thee,
Good Prince; please treat our inn as your own home.
Your luggage I will bring to you forthwith.
To host so eminent a personage
Is just the hostelry we hope to be.
You lend our halls a grace and dignity.

ORENTHAL. Your kindness is most welcome here this morn.
The red-eye flight has me a little worn.
Hop to! Now stow my clubs! I'll need them soon.
First, from the front desk, I'll secure my room.

BELLHOP. Of course, good Prince, your wishes we'll fulfill.
I see you aim to hit the links this day,
May slices, hooks, and shanks plague thee no more,
As Chi-town greens and fairways you explore.

ORENTHAL. Just modest skill hath I with golfing sticks,
But I assure you I will take my licks.
But first to bed and slumber soft,
My beauty sleep cannot be lost.

THE TRAGEDY OF ORENTHAL

[Aside.]
Away, and mock the time with fairest show:
False face must hide what the false heart doth know.[20]

BELLHOP. Prince Juice, a gracious favor I do beg,
I must confess I long have been a fan.
If autograph I missed, I'd soon regret,
Most humbly I entreat, a signature?

ORENTHAL. With willing heart I'll gladly sign for thee:
"Prince Juice, with warm regards."

BELLHOP. Most gracious Prince, I swell with happiness,
My sincere gratitude I give to thee!

ORENTHAL. Thou art most welcome, of that I am sure.

[Aside.]
Such adulation leaves me numb and cold,
Dark thoughts about the murders still unfold.

DESK CLERK. Your room is ready, you'll be glad to learn,
Call me, dear Prince, for any small concern.
Thy slightest wish we quickly will attend,
For thee, most lavish effort we'll expend.

ORENTHAL. Good sir, some sleep is all that I do need,
My stay will not your other plans impede,
Just rouse me with a wake-up call at noon,
So I can rise for tee time none too soon.

MICHAEL W. MONK

Desk Clerk. I will myself be conscious of your nest.
I will ensure a quiet, peaceful rest.

Orenthal. Just peace and solitude are all I seek,
You'll find me just a guest, most mild and meek.

Orenthal proceeds to his hotel room. Exeunt all others.

Orenthal. Thank God at last I have some solitude,
The first I am alone since Rockingham.
To pose as carefree star upon a lark,
Hath been a painful burden since her death,
This deed unshapes me quite; makes me unpregnant
And dull to all proceedings. A beheaded maid;
And by an eminent body, that enforc'd
His law against it! But that her tender shame
Will not proclaim against her being's loss,
How might they tongue me!
Yet reason dares them no,
For my notoriety bears so credent bulk
That no particular scandal once can touch,
But it confounds me now that
Goldman should have lived
Save that his riotous youth, with dangerous sense,
Did rashly seek to take such quick revenge.
Alack, when once our grace we have forgot,
Nothing goes right; we would, and we would not.[21]

THE TRAGEDY OF ORENTHAL

Orenthal enters the bathroom in his room.

My finger's cut continueth to bleed,
I must imagine how this wound occurred.
Look, how I rub my hands to wash them
   clean,
It's become an accustom'd action with me!
What, will these hands ne'er be clean? Here's
   a spot!
Out damned spot! Out, I say!—Hell is murky.[22]
Exhaustion overcomes me, like a weight,
Since just an hour's sleep methinks I've had
In hours even more than twenty-four.
But slumber doth elude me on the bed,
And wide awake, my tired mind doth race.
Just when will they the bodies stumble on?
When will they find my dear Nicole is gone?

Exit.

ACT III

SCENE 1

(Bundy condominium of Princess Nicole, Monday, June 13, 1994, at 5:00 a.m.)

Enter Constables Lange, Vannatter, Fuhrman, and Phillips.

LANGE. This bloody crime scene we have now surveyed:
It's surely not an average robbery
That's followed by a furtive cut and run.
No! Stabbed and mutilated were these souls!
With rage their throats have savagely been slashed.
Such carnage by some maniac deranged,
Or else, perchance, cold personal revenge.

VANNATTER. I am the twenty-sixth policeman here,
Yet I can't fathom all that this doth mean.

FUHRMAN. And I the seventeenth to sign the log.
Our job is now to double-check the scene.

PHILLIPS. Fifteen officers, too, preceded me,
Before the butchered bodies I did see.

LANGE. Let's summarize the matters we've observed
And evidence intriguing we have found:
Two human bodies sleeping the big sleep,
Two bloody sets of shoe prints on the walk,
A dark knit cap and bloody left-hand glove,

The glove lay near the body of the man.
Five drops of blood just to the left of path
The killer likely took to flee the scene.
These drops we will with science analyze;
They could confirm the killer if we're wise.

PHILLIPS.　We've tentatively now identified
The woman slain upon the grass outside,
With help from local neighbors who have said
They know the prostrate female who lies dead.
They say she is Prince Orenthal's ex-wife,
So brutally deprived of her young life.

VANNATTER.　And now Commander Bushey doth request
That we inform the Prince that she is slain,
"As soon as humanly it's possible,"
Before the media doth him besiege.
With Orenthal we must coordinate
So he can take his children home with him.

LANGE.　The four of us must seek the Prince at once,
To meet him and convey the somber tale.
We'll seek cooperation from the Prince,
For background information we will need.
Perhaps the killer he can help us find,
Perhaps this knot of riddles help unwind.

Exeunt.

THE TRAGEDY OF ORENTHAL

SCENE 2
(Orenthal's Brentwood estate, Monday, June 13, 1994, at 5:15 a.m.)

Enter Constables Vannatter, Lange, Fuhrman, and Phillips.

VANNATTER. Strange matters are afoot at Rockingham,
Access to the estate we cannot gain.
We'll add this up and see what we have here:
The lights are on inside the house,
And cars in the driveway certainly.
Though Simpson, and his maid,
Inside are supposed to be,
They answer not the phone
Or come to intercom.
The Bronco's parked askew,
It's at an angle strange,
One tire is on the curb,
As if 'twas parked in haste.
And on the Bronco's door handle there's
   blood—
Yes, blood is on the handle, driver's side.

LANGE. Something's wrong.
Lights on,
Cars everywhere,
No one answering.
Are Simpson and his maid in trouble here?
Their safety we must posthaste now ensure.

FUHRMAN. I'll scale the wall should you advise.

VANNATTER. Indeed proceed; we have but little choice,
The perpetrator may have been here, too.

Fuhrman scales the wall and opens the gate for constables.

PHILLIPS. The doorbell we do ring, on door we knock,
Yet silence is the only thing we hear.
Let's check the bungalows I see in back.

FUHRMAN. I think someone's inside this bungalow;
I'll rap upon the door so we shall know.

Enter Kato Kaelin, emerging from first bungalow.

KAELIN. What matter presses so?
Why pound you on my door?

PHILLIPS. We're from LAPD—just who are you?

KAELIN. I'm clept Kato Kaelin.
I do resideth here.
What matter is amiss?
I plead unto your ear.

PHILLIPS. Prince Orenthal we seek, with news of woe.

KAELIN. I think the Prince is not upon the grounds.
Arnelle, the Prince's daughter, lives next door,
Prince Juice and his location she can tell.

Enter Arnelle, the Prince's daughter, who has been roused.

THE TRAGEDY OF ORENTHAL

ARNELLE. How now! Who doth disturb my quiet peace?

PHILLIPS. Are you the offspring of the absent Prince?

ARNELLE. I claim that honor. Who the hell are you?

LANGE. We're from LAPD with news of woe.
Know you the long-haired lad who's standing there?

ARNELLE. I do, it's Kato Kaelin, who lives here.

LANGE. Who drives the Bronco parked out on the street?

ARNELLE. The Prince, my father, drives that set of wheels.

VANNATTER. Where would the Prince be on this early morn?

ARNELLE. I think inside the main house he should be;
Have not you tried yourself the Prince to see?

VANNATTER. No answer we received when we did knock.

ARNELLE. The key for you I shall forthwith procure.

Arnelle and constables enter main house.

VANNATTER. Neat order in the maid's room I observe;
No evidence of struggle or misdeed.

FUHRMAN. Come list' to what this Kaelin has to say;
His information may show us the way.

KAELIN.   His Bentley to McDonald's we did take,
          The Prince did want some take-out food last eve.
          He ate his food as we did drive back here,
          My food I saved to eat when we returned.
          About 9:30 here we did arrive.
          But then, about 10:45 I heard
          A loud noise from behind the bungalow,
          The cause of which, forsooth, I did not know.
          I heard three thumps, and feared an
             earthquake's wrath,
          A picture frame did dance upon the wall.
          I went outside and saw a limousine,
          The driver for the Prince said he did wait,
          For LAX, he said Prince Juice was late.

LANGE.   *[Addressing Princess Arnelle.]*
          A grisly message I must give to you,
          Forgive that I must be the messenger:
          Nicole, she has been murdered at her home.

          Arnelle breaks down, screaming and crying.

ARNELLE. I gotta call A.C. I gotta call A.C.
          He will provide some aid. I fear it's up to me!

LANGE.   And what of this "A.C."
          Of whom you speak to me?

ARNELLE. Al Cowlings is of whom I speak,
          The Prince's bosom friend.

PHILLIPS. Let's focus on our first priority:
          Prince Juice I must now call immediately.

> He must not hear this horror from the press.
> We surely owe him such small courtesy.

Exeunt.

SCENE 3
(Prince Orenthal's Chicago hotel room and Bundy estate)

Enter Orenthal; telephone rings.

ORENTHAL. Hello?

PHILLIPS. Good morrow, is this *the* Prince Orenthal?

ORENTHAL. Yes, Orenthal I am, and who is this?

PHILLIPS. Detective Phillips from LAPD,
With information I must now convey:
As matter first, thy children are quite well,
But other morbid news I must now give:
The Princess, your Nicole, she has been killed.

ORENTHAL. Oh my God! Nicole is killed?
Oh my God! Is she dead?

PHILLIPS. Good Prince, you must contain your grief, I pray,
We have your children at LAPD.
We seek your counsel. Who should pick them up?

ORENTHAL. What sayest thou? My children you did take?
You speak as if they're in your custody.

PHILLIPS.   Arnelle, your daughter, wants to speak with thee.
            No other one was there to care for them,
            So we did take them where they're safe from
              harm.
            From thee, good Prince, we seek instructions
              clear.

ORENTHAL.   Then with alacrity I will fly home.
            Yes, I must to the coast with quick dispatch.
            Return I will, as fast just as I can.
            Perhaps she can assist both you and me.

            Arnelle speaks with Orenthal.

PHILLIPS.   [Aside.]
            No details doth he seek about her death,
            Not even simple questions: How? Or why?
            Although he did express an open grief,
            Why doth he not inquire of circumstance?

            Orenthal hangs up telephone.

ORENTHAL.   They'll circle me like vultures all too soon,
            Swooping in and smelling for the blood,
            I cannot show a weakness or a doubt.
            Friends I'll consult, and lawyers, for advice.
            To all I must contend I'm innocent,
            Since after all, this really wasn't me.
            She forced a demon rise within my head,
            Who did a deed that I could never do.
            'Twas really someone else who used a knife,
            The real Prince Juice would never take a life.
            If it were really I who murdered her,

THE TRAGEDY OF ORENTHAL

> 'Twould gnaw upon my heart forevermore.
> But I must now create some evidence
> That I'm distraught: I'll break a water glass,
> Indeed to reap a double benefit:
> By breaking glass upon my finger's cut,
> Exacerbating smaller current wound.
> I'll make a bloody stain upon the towel,
> Which will so palpably confirm my grief.
> 'Twould be an act believable to all,
> And demonstrate what loss and pain I feel.
> Whatever pain this new cut doth demand,
> I'll have an answer for my bloody hand.

Orenthal breaks a hotel water glass, further cutting the middle finger of his left hand.

ORENTHAL. Only Kato Kaelin saw my finger bleed last night.
He won't blow my cover, but will testify I'm right.

Exit.

SCENE 4
(The kitchen of Orenthal's Rockingham estate)

Enter Constables Lange, Vannatter, Fuhrman, and Phillips.

LANGE. Nicole Brown's parents next must be informed.
Before the herds of media stampede.
Full ninety minutes drive they are from here.

Reluctantly, I'll notify by phone,
Prompt notification hath more import,
Than niceties of meeting face to face.
The Browns' phone number Arnelle hath supplied,
A gruesome task, to tell a child hath died.

*Lange calls the Browns from the kitchen telephone.
Enter Denise Brown, Lou Brown, Juditha Brown,
and Dominique Brown.*

Lou Brown. Hello, who speaks to me?

Lange. I am Detective Lange, LAPD.
Is this Nicole Brown's parents' residence?

Lou Brown. It is, and to her father you do speak.

Lange. With solemn sorrow, I must you inform
Your daughter has been killed at her abode.

Denise Brown. *[Listening in.]*
I knew that motherfucker would kill her!
O.J. did it! I know O.J. did it!
That son of a bitch killed her as I feared!

Juditha Brown and Brown Sisters. O.J. did it! O.J. did it! O.J. did it!

Lange. Your grandchildren are safe and out of harm;
Arnelle will pick them up and bring them here.

THE TRAGEDY OF ORENTHAL

JUDITHA BROWN.   I beg thee please forgive my sobs and tears,
But I do need to speak of this to you.
'Twas just last night we supped with Princess Nic
At Mezzaluna Brentwood restaurant,
We went to toast and Sydney celebrate.
And the recital, Orenthal was there,
But did not join us at the restaurant.

LANGE.   I thank thee for thy thoughts in moment bleak,
Most soon I promise we will further speak.

Lange ends phone call to the Browns.

Exeunt Browns.

Enter Fuhrman, coming from outside.

FUHRMAN.   Come quickly, you must see what I hath found
In narrow pathway back of bungalow.

LANGE.   Pray, show the way to that of which thou
    speakst.

FUHRMAN.   Behind the bungalow where Kato dwells
I shall illuminate with flashlight bright,
Please look below the air conditioner:
An object shrouded near the shrubbery.

VANNATTER.   Forsooth! It seems a bloodstained leather glove,
Appearing moist with sticky crimson hue.
And further it right-handed seems to be.
At first blush it appears to be a mate
To left-hand glove that's at the murder scene.

As with all evidence, we dare not touch,
If this glove is a mate, it's just too much.
Constable Fuhrman, fly to Bundy now
And mark the other glove—is it a match?
Both gloves we needs must quickly photograph.

LANGE. This stunning piece of evidence suggests
Connections 'tween the deed and this estate.

VANNATTER. Could Orenthal a suspect be?

LANGE. The Princess's own sister doth agree,
She screamed his name almost immediately.

VANNATTER. The Prince? Good Orenthal? A murderer?

LANGE. I see his friend, Al Cowlings, hath arrived,
And indicated he would Arnelle drive
To West LA Division Headquarters
To pick up youthful offspring of the Prince.
He nothing more whatever had to speak,
About this matter acted very meek.
A word of greeting or of sympathy,
Would seem much more appropriate to me.

Exeunt Fuhrman and Phillips.

LANGE. The nature of this murder starts to form:
The left-hand glove is ripped off in the fray
By dead man who lay butchered at the scene.
The killer then sustained a bloody cut
To his left hand no longer with a glove,
Which injury did drip five bloody drops

                Just to the left of exiting shoe prints:
                A bloody calling card for us to read.

VANNATTER.   A possible scenario,
                Based upon the facts we know.

LANGE.   Away I am to Bundy to explore,
                While you each inch of Rockingham peruse.

                Exit Lange.

VANNATTER.   The telling glove in back now changes all,
                Directly implicating this locale.
                A warrant I will need to search this house,
                But first the criminologist I'll meet,
                So he can photograph the glove and car.
                And dawn's first rosy cheek now starts to peek
                And this estate illuminate a bit.

                Vannatter walks to the Bronco, parked askew.

                Indeed the Bronco I can better view.
                Good God, a blood smear on the driver's door,
                And smears are on the console in the truck.
                Stand, ho, I see some blood drops on the
                    street!
                I'll trace these very blood drops I have found,
                Determine where they lead upon the ground.

                Vannatter follows blood to driveway in front of estate.

                My heavens! Orenthal could be the one!
                While close examination must proceed,

Straight to the house the trail of blood doth lead,
The blood that guides me to the Prince's door
May be involved with murder's grisly gore.

Enter Arnelle and Cowlings with Sydney and Justin Simpson.

So swift Arnelle and Cowlings hath returned,
With children of the Prince they duck inside.
The constables that swarm this sprawling
   nest,
Suggest a weighty problem at the least,
But silently they slink into the house.
No questions do they ask, or comments make.
Canst they suspect Prince Juice could be the one
To mercilessly slay his former bride?
What a thought for a daughter to endure:
Her pater now a murderer impure.
Or doth she know already of his deed,
And now his next instructions start to heed?
Some daughters would recoil disgustedly,
While others would accomplice quickly be,
And fix their mind to try to keep him free.

Enter Furhman, returning from Bundy with photographer.

FUHRMAN.   A photograph we've taken demonstrates,
The gloves do clearly seem to be a match:
The same dark color, style identical,
Though brand name cannot yet be ascertained,
When we later move the gloves, we can compare.

THE TRAGEDY OF ORENTHAL

VANNATTER. A bloody path doth lead to Simpson's gate
I will seal off completely all these grounds.
Assiduously, blood we must preserve,
This horrid mess doth no less care deserve.

Exeunt.

SCENE 5
*(Interrogation room, LAPD Parker Center Facility,
Monday, June 13, 1994, at 1:35 p.m.)*

Enter Constables Lange and Vannatter, and Orenthal.

VANNATTER. June 13th, 1994, it is.
The time is afternoon: 1:35.
As interview doth formally commence,
Orenthal James Simpson sits with us.
What date didst thou spring from thy
mother's loins?

ORENTHAL. I drew first breath on 7th of July,
And 1947 was the year.

VANNATTER. Before we talk, I must disclaimer make
Of rights you have, so Constitutional:
To remain silent you possess the right,
But if that right you do decide to waive,
Your statements can and will be used 'gainst you,
In court of law or other legal stage.
Thou hast the right to speak with lawyer, too.

                    And right to counsel while the questions fly.
                    If an attorney you cannot afford,
                    You can have state's attorney without charge.
                    Do you your rights completely understand?

ORENTHAL.   Yes, I do.

VANNATTER.   Do you then clearly wish to yield your right
                    So silent to remain?

ORENTHAL.   I do.

VANNATTER.   And do attorney, too, you wish to waive?

ORENTHAL.   I do.

VANNATTER.   We are investigating, obviously,
                    The death of your ex-wife and another man.
                    Are you indeed divorced from her right now?

ORENTHAL.   Yes, of course.

VANNATTER.   How many years since marriage split in twain?

ORENTHAL.   Two years ago she ceased to be my bride.

VANNATTER.   How fared things then twixt thee and she
                    In times that followed that selfsame divorce?

ORENTHAL.   A reconciliation we had sought,
                    Which effort finally seemed to be for naught.
                    'Twas nearly four full seasons of the year
                    We did attempt to patch the ruptured tear.

THE TRAGEDY OF ORENTHAL

	But we somehow knew that it would not work, With both of us the doubt did clearly lurk. We did agree to part three weeks ago So each of us our separate ways could know.
VANNATTER.	Is it true that the two children are yours?
ORENTHAL.	They are.
LANGE.	Did their late mother retain custody?
ORENTHAL.	The custody was joint for her and me.
LANGE.	Was custody decided by the courts?
ORENTHAL.	Yes, through the courts and all the legal things, We had no problems with the kids, We do everything together, you know, With our kids.
VANNATTER.	Didst the first separation cause thee pain? Did the divorce cause problems for you two?
ORENTHAL.	I loved her, didn't want to separate.
VANNATTER.	What of the crime reports Nicole hath filed?
ORENTHAL.	Some years ago, an ugly spat ensued On New Year's Eve, and she filed a report. And then an altercation one year back, Which wasn't any physical dispute; I just kicked in her door, or something else.

VANNATTER. So these occasions caused police reports?

ORENTHAL. Forsooth, they did.
I didst remain and talked to the police.

LANGE. Did not one case result in your arrest?

ORENTHAL. After the New Year's spat, now years gone by,
Community service I did complete.

VANNATTER. Did not this matter involve your arrest?

ORENTHAL. Arrested? No, I never really was.

VANNATTER. I need to ask you, when did you last sleep?

ORENTHAL. I slept a little on the plane, not much.

VANNATTER. When was the last time that you saw Nicole?

ORENTHAL. At dance recital, I did see her last;
She left, and with her parents I didst speak.

VANNATTER. When did the dance recital terminate?

ORENTHAL. About 6:30, close as I can state.

VANNATTER. And they departed for the dinner date?

ORENTHAL. Her mother, father, sisters, and my kids
Proceeded to a dinner gathering.
Nicole's Jeep Cherokee did transport some
And others in her sister's second car.

THE TRAGEDY OF ORENTHAL

VANNATTER. What car didst thou drive to thy daughter's dance?

ORENTHAL. It was, I think, my Bentley that I drove.

VANNATTER. Dost thou own the Ford Bronco at your house?

ORENTHAL. Hertz owns it,
And Hertz lets me use it, too.

VANNATTER. So it's your Bronco parked upon the street?

ORENTHAL. Mmm-hmm.
I drive it and housekeeper does, too.
You know, it's kind of—

VANNATTER. An all-purpose vehicle?

ORENTHAL. All-purpose, yeah, that's what I meant to say,
The only car the others all can drive,
Pursuant to insurance rules and jive.

LANGE. And when did thou last drive this Bronco truck?

ORENTHAL. 'Twas yesterday, if I recall with luck.

LANGE. What time of day, when you say yesterday?

ORENTHAL. In the morning, in the afternoon.

VANNATTER. Okay, let's start when the recital ends,
Which you have placed at roughly 6:30.
She left, and then you with her parents spoke?

ORENTHAL. Her mother asked if I could dine with them,
I said no thanks.

VANNATTER. Where went you from there?

ORENTHAL. Ah, home—home for a while—got my car.
For a while, tried to find my girlfriend
For a while, came back to the house.

VANNATTER. So what time did you physically get home?

ORENTHAL. Seven-something.

VANNATTER. Seven-something?
And then you left and what?

ORENTHAL. Yeah, I'm trying to think, now did I leave?
You know, I'm always—I had to run and get
My daughter flowers. I was actually doing the
  recital,
So I rushed and got her some flowers,
Then I came home and Paula I did call,
As I was going over to her house,
And Paula wasn't home.

VANNATTER. This Paula stands as girlfriend now to you?

ORENTHAL. That piece of information's very true.

VANNATTER. What last name did you say that Paula bears?

ORENTHAL. 'Tis Barbieri, though I did not say.

THE TRAGEDY OF ORENTHAL

VANNATTER. So Barbieri you saw not last night?

ORENTHAL. No, we'd been to an affair the night before,
And then I came back home, basically at home.
I mean anytime I was—whatever the time
It took me to get to the recital,
And back, to get to the flower shop and back,
I mean, that's the time I was out of the house.

VANNATTER. What time did you then leave for the airport?

ORENTHAL. About—the limo was supposed to come at 10:45.
Normally, they get there a little earlier.
I was rushing around—somewhere between
   there and 11.

LANGE. And what time did the plane take off last night?

ORENTHAL. At quarter to midnight it did soar high.

LANGE. So yesterday you drove the white Bronco?

ORENTHAL. Mmm-hmm.

LANGE. And where then did you park it at your house?

ORENTHAL. The first time probably by the mailbox,
I'm trying to think—did I bring it inside
On driveway? Normally I park outside.

LANGE. Where, yesterday, the last time did you park?

ORENTHAL. Right where it is.

LANGE.	Where it is now?
ORENTHAL.	Yeah, right there on the street, on Rockingham.
LANGE.	And what time did you park the Bronco there?
ORENTHAL.	Eight-something, seven . . . eight . . . nine o'clock, I don't know, right in that area.
LANGE.	To dance recital, Bronco did you drive?
ORENTHAL.	No. Like I said, I came home, I got my car, To see selfsame girlfriend I did embark.
LANGE.	So you drove the Bentley home and then you took The Bronco to drive to another place?
ORENTHAL.	In the Bronco, 'cause in my Bronco was the phone. And because it's a Bronco, It's a Bronco, it's what I drive, you know. I'd rather drive it than any other car. And you know, as I was going over there, I called a couple times, and she's not there. So I left her a message on the phone, And I checked my messages, there were none. She wasn't there and she may have left town. Then I came back, ended up with Kato.
LANGE.	Again, what time didst thou the Bronco park?
ORENTHAL.	Eight-something, maybe. Jacuzzi we'd not done,

THE TRAGEDY OF ORENTHAL

                We went and got a burger, just us two,
                And I'd come home and kind of leisurely
                Got ready to go.

LANGE.   And in no hurry whilst thou parked the Bronco?

ORENTHAL.   No.

LANGE.   The reason that I asked is just because
                The Bronco I saw parked, it was askew.

ORENTHAL.   Well, it's parked because . . .
                I don't know that it's at an angle strange.
                It's parked because . . .
                Well, I was hustling at the end of day
                To get my stuff, my phone, and everything,
                So when I pulled the truck out of the gate,
                A tight turn I did have to navigate.

LANGE.   So in the compound you did drive the truck?

ORENTHAL.   That's right: to get my stuff all out of it,
                And then I put it out and ran inside,
                Before the gate did close upon my hide.

VANNATTER.   How suffered you the wound upon your hand?

ORENTHAL.   I don't know.
                The first time, when I was in Chicago and all,
                But at the house I was just running around.

VANNATTER.   How did you cut your hand in Chicago?

ORENTHAL. I broke a glass when one of you did call,
I guess I just went bonkers for a bit.

VANNATTER. Didst thou cut it first that way?

ORENTHAL. Mmm, I do believe that it was cut before,
But I think I did open it again.

LANGE. Do you remember bleeding in the truck?

ORENTHAL. I know that I did bleed inside my house,
And then from Bronco I retrieved the phone.

LANGE. Mmm-hmm. And just where is the phone
right now?

ORENTHAL. It's here with me, right here inside my bag.

LANGE. So do you now recall bleeding at all?

ORENTHAL. Well, I mean I was bleeding, no big deal,
I bleed all the time.
Since I play golf and stuff, I tend to bleed;
Nicks and stuff are always here and there.

LANGE. And for the nick what first aid did you take?
When did you place that Band-Aid on the cut?

ORENTHAL. I asked the girl this morning for something.

LANGE. And did the girl a remedy provide?

ORENTHAL. She did, because last night I left in haste,

	And Kato had said something else to me And I was rushing to secure my phone, I put a little something on it then.
LANGE.	When were you at Nicole's house the last time?
ORENTHAL.	I don't go in—I won't go in her house. I haven't been in her house in a week, Or maybe five days I think it has been. I go to her house quite an awfully lot, I'm always dropping off the kids and such Picking up the kids, Fooling around with the dog, you know.
VANNATTER.	But never hast gone in the house you say?
ORENTHAL.	Until five days, six days ago, that's right. While dating Paula, leave Nicole alone. Hath been the wisdom I have surely known.
VANNATTER.	Prince Juice, it seems some matters are amiss: We've got some blood that's on and in your car. And blood that's at your house.
ORENTHAL.	Well, draw my blood for test if you demand!
VANNATTER.	We will, but just when did you cut your hand?
ORENTHAL.	The cut, as I did say, occurred last night. Somewhere when I was rushing to my flight.
VANNATTER.	You say the cut was post-recital time?

ORENTHAL.   I do believe so, yes.

VANNATTER.   You say of late you sought to reconcile?

ORENTHAL.   That's right, but our attempts did not bear fruit,
             A fortnight and one-half ago we split;
             We decided the hell with it, you know.

VANNATTER.   So barely three weeks past you were with her?

ORENTHAL.   It's, it's—seeing her again, yeah, I mean, yeah.
             We've not had sex for over two full months,
             For offspring we had tried to reconcile.

VANNATTER.   How long were you together with Nicole?

ORENTHAL.   Ten years, then seven more, if truth be told.

VANNATTER.   And didst thou ever strike her, Orenthal?

ORENTHAL.   Ah, one night it is true there was a scene.
             We had a fight and she did smite me hard.
             They never seemed to want to hear my side,
             They always let her take them for a ride.
             Nicole was drunk, and she tore up my house,
             I didn't hit her, but now I'm the louse.

VANNATTER.   So you just slapped her face a couple times?

ORENTHAL.   No, no. I wrestled her is what I did.
             I didn't slap her any way at all.
             Since then she's hit me quite a few more times,
             But never have I touched her after that.

THE TRAGEDY OF ORENTHAL

LANGE.   O.J., what are your thoughts on polygraph?
                     I know we've talked about it once before.

ORENTHAL.   I'll tell you now my thoughts on all of that.
                     Eventually I'd like to wear that hat,
                     But now I harbor thoughts so strangely weird,
                     I've thoughts I fear I care not to admit.
                     When you've been with a person for so long,
                     Years seventeen are not a short-lived song.
                     I must full understand this polygraph,
                     If it's true blue, I'll gladly pledge my staff.

LANGE.   Well, you are not required to take the test.

ORENTHAL.   If for elimination this test works,
                     My lawyer's consultation I will seek.

LANGE.   We're talking to you since you're the ex-spouse.

ORENTHAL.   I know that I'm now target number one,
                     Since you advise of blood pointing to me.

LANGE.   Is it your blood we have upon the drive?
                     And what of blood discovered in the house?

ORENTHAL.   If it is dripped, it is what I did drip
                     When hurrying to make my airport trip.

LANGE.   That was last night after the recital
                     When you were rushing frantically around?

ORENTHAL.   Forsooth, I did not know that I did bleed
                     Until I saw it at my kitchen sink,

	Then grabbed I up a napkin for the cut,
	And never thought about it after that.
LANGE.	When was the last time that you saw Nicole?
ORENTHAL.	The last time I saw Nicole, physically,
	I saw her obviously last night,
	And before that I cannot say just when.
LANGE.	We'll close and now will photograph your hand
	And assay all of this to understand.

Exeunt.

SCENE 6
(Lange's office, Monday, June 13, 1994, at 3:30 p.m.)

Enter Lange and Vannatter.

LANGE.	A most revealing moment with the Prince.
	He stammered and he stuttered forth methinks,
	Most hesitant, vague, not at all forthright,
	I would have liked to've seen his acts last night.
VANNATTER.	He bobbed and weaved, and most defensive was,
	He feigned at first the Bronco was of Hertz,
	And that he never ventured in her house,
	'Twas she indeed that waxed so physical,
	He'd have us think he was the one abused.
LANGE.	He seemed uneasy with the blood we found,

THE TRAGEDY OF ORENTHAL

                Though he did offer up a bloody test.
                To claim "I always bleed" doth not ring true,
                That tested my credulity anew.

VANNATTER.   At times he claims to leisurely proceed,
                Thereafter, all's alacrity and speed,
                If nothing he was doing on this eve,
                Why hurry to the limo for reprieve?

LANGE.   He acteth not like one who's wrongly blamed.
                The guiltless lambs recoil at hint of guilt,
                With righteousness that's born of innocence.
                But he, like guilty puppy, hangs his head.
                No outrage for her loss doth he display,
                He rendeth not the clothing, nor the hair.

VANNATTER.   With evidence collected on this date,
                His history of violence to his mate,
                The waffling interview sans alibi,
                Could we have now identified our guy?
                Dost thou think we've enough to seek arrest?
                Or thinkest thou deliberation best?

LANGE.   A night is but small breath and little pause
                To answer matters of this consequence.[23]

Exeunt.

SCENE 7
(Orenthal's estate, Friday, June 17, 1994)

Enter Orenthal and Cowlings.

ORENTHAL. Investigation rumbles forth apace,
The glacier doth creep closer day by day,
It chills my mental state to contemplate
Arrest's dark specter looming at my door.

COWLINGS. But what if you ignore what's behind the door?
What if you seek a distant hidden clime?
To flee the rude indictments and much more,
Arrangements must be planned, you've little
time.

ORENTHAL. Bloody instructions, which being taught, return
To plague the inventor: this even-handed justice
Commends th'ingredience of our poison'd
chalice
To our own lips.[24]

COWLINGS. Come, come, my Grace, no need to talk of such,
You've options more than suicide to touch.

ORENTHAL. But if I live, my life will haunted be,
The crowds will swarm and fingers point at me;
Or worse I'll be some miscreant's dessert,
Inside a grimy prison cell be hurt.
If I cannot avoid such cursed life,
Macabre thoughts of death come from such
strife.
Enough of this, I can no longer wait.

Let's off to Bob Kardashian's estate.
I've packed some things to take along with me
That will provide a bit of privacy.

COWLINGS.   Of course, my Lord, I'll now with you away,
We'll try to keep the constables at bay.

Exeunt.

SCENE 8
(LAPD press conference)

Enter police brass, Constables Gascon and Vannatter, and reporters.

GASCON.   I speak for LAPD here today,
We've carefully examined many facts,
And witnesses they're many we have tapped,
Both here and in Chicago we have looked,
And, based upon the same, we have obtained
A warrant for Prince Orenthal's arrest:
For murders of Nicole Brown Simpson and
Ronald Lyle Goldman he will stand.
This morning he was scheduled to appear,
He failed to show and he has fled, we fear.
The LAPD hath commenced a search,
For Orenthal, wherever he doth perch.

Exeunt.

SCENE 9
(Press conference with Orenthal's counselors)

Enter counselors Shapiro and Kardashian, and reporters. Shapiro steps to the microphone.

SHAPIRO. O.J., I pray, wherever you may be,
For the sake of your dearest family,
For the sake of children you have spawned,
Please surrender now, immediately,
Surrender to the law enforcement man,
Surrender just as quickly as you can.

KARDASHIAN. If your attention I may have, forsooth,
I'll read to you a letter from the Prince,
A missive penned today before he fled,
Please lend an ear to things that he has said:

Kardashian reads Orenthal's letter.

"To whom it may concern:
First understand I didn't kill Nicole,
I loved her much too much the truth to tell.
We mutually agreed to separate,
An amicable pact we reached of late,
Unlike what has been written in the press
A great relationship we had: the best.
On New Year's '89 I took the heat,
When told that it would still the press's beat,
But, as a last wish, press, I do beseech,
Please, please, don't for my precious children reach.
Their lives will soon be tough enough, I'm sure,

> Please let them live in peace, with hearts secure.
> In life I've mostly done the proper things,
> I can't go on with what the future brings.
> No matter what, they all will look and point,
> With this nightmare, I'll not my kids anoint.
> This way, they can just go on with their lives,
> Again, good journalists, let them survive.
> I'm sorry for the Goldman family,
> I know how much it hurts, you can trust me.
> And please do not feel sorry now for me.
> I've had a great life, great friends, all can see.
> Please think of the real O.J.
> And not this lost person.
> Thanks for making my life special.
> I hope I helped yours.
> Peace and love,
> O.J."

Exeunt.

SCENE 10
(LAPD Robbery-Homicide Division)

Enter Lange and Vannatter, watching Shapiro and Kardashian press conference on television.

LANGE. Good God, I think he's going to kill himself
A good-bye letter placed upon the shelf.

VANNATTER. It seems to me admission of his guilt,
Into his speech no sorrow hath he built,

Himself he doth so clearly, dearly love,
Into his head he'll ne'er a bullet shove.
In this small world he'll find no place to hide,
But he will not engage in suicide.

Exeunt.

SCENE 11
(Nicole's grave)

Enter Orenthal, who talks to Nicole's grave.

ORENTHAL. I've left my note confirming suicide,
But now I bring my leaden heart to you.
How I am punish'd with sore distraction.
What I have done, I here proclaim was madness.
Was't Orenthal wrong'd Nicole? Never
   Orenthal.
If Orenthal from himself be ta'en away,
And when he's not himself does wrong Nicole,
Then Orenthal does it not, Orenthal denies it.
Who does it, then? His madness: if't be so,
Orenthal is of the faction that is wrong'd;
His madness is poor Orenthal's enemy.
Sweet Nicole, in this audience,
Let my disclaiming from a purpos'd evil
Free me so far in your most generous thoughts,
That I have shot mine arrow o'er the house
And hurt my lover.[25]

Exit.

THE TRAGEDY OF ORENTHAL

SCENE 12

(Orenthal's Bronco, heading north on 405 Freeway)

        Enter Orenthal and Cowlings, with Cowlings driving the Bronco.

ORENTHAL. Had I but died an hour before her death,
I had liv'd a blessed time; for, from this instant,
There's nothing serious in mortality;
All is but toys: renown, and grace, is dead;
The wine of life is drawn, and the mere lees
Is left this vault to brag of.[26]
Ere I will eat my meal in fear, and sleep
In the affliction of these terrible dreams,
That shake me nightly. Better I be with the dead,
Whom I, to gain my peace, have sent to peace,
Than on the torture of the mind to lie
In restless ecstasy. Nicole is in her grave;
After life's fitful fever she sleeps well.[27]

COWLINGS. How now! I see police upon our tail!
The game is up, we've been identified.
The license plate must have been recognized
Or visage seen by knowing motorist.

ORENTHAL. Stop not! Drive on! Continueth, my friend!
I'll let them not my body rend.
They'll shy from using violence on us,
If slowly we proceed without a fuss.

        Orenthal's cellphone rings with a call from Constable Lange.

85

MICHAEL W. MONK

Enter Lange.

LANGE. Hello, O.J.? Is this Orenthal here?
'Tis I, Constable Lange, who hath your ear.

ORENTHAL. Just let me get back to my house, I pray,
Where I lived with Nicole one distant day.

LANGE. We're going to let you drive to your estate,
Just throw the gun away for safety's sake.

ORENTHAL. This gun is not to keep you guys away,
This gun is here for me to end my day.

LANGE. Nobody's going to hurt you, throw the gun.

ORENTHAL. The gun is just for me, for I am done.

LANGE. Please realize you're scaring everyone.

ORENTHAL. Just tell them that I'm sorry later on,
I'm sorry I did this to the police.

LANGE. I would not wish to tell that to your kids.

ORENTHAL. To children, I've already said good-bye,
For that cruel job, I'll not on you rely.

LANGE. Think of your children and then contemplate,
You'll see your family back at the estate.
Please throw the gun away for safety's sake.
No injuries to anyone you'll make.

THE TRAGEDY OF ORENTHAL

ORENTHAL.   Aah—aooooh—aaaaah.
I'm the only one that deserves—

LANGE.   No, you don't deserve that.

ORENTHAL.   I'm going to get hurt.

LANGE.   Sweet Prince, you do not deserve to get hurt.
Sweet Prince, you do not deserve to get hurt.

ORENTHAL.   Aah—aooooh—aaaaah.
All I did was love Nicole, that's all,
All I did was love her, I recall.
I do love everybody, large or small.
My love I could not anyway forestall.

LANGE.   Tomorrow a brighter day will make,
Just ditch the gun for safety's sake.

ORENTHAL.   Aah—aooooh—aaaaah.
I'm just going to go with Nicole,
That's all I'm gonna do.
That's all I'm trying to do.
I couldn't do it in a field.
I went to do it at her grave.
I want to do it at my house.

LANGE.   You're not going to do anything, O.J.
Too many people love you, I must say.

ORENTHAL.   My house that swarms with guns please do alert,
And tell the cops that them I will not hurt.

LANGE. Your words I will most carefully convey
These fears I can completely now allay.

ORENTHAL. 'Twas the first date that I had with Nicole,
The first night we went out just for a stroll.
We went back to my house on that first date,
And newly purchased, shambles was the state.

LANGE. Ah-haa.

ORENTHAL. That's where we were, and happy were we there.

LANGE. You've now almost arrived at your estate,
Please throw the gun away, for safety's sake.

ORENTHAL. The steely pistol will strike only me,
And others will no harm have cause to see.

LANGE. If thou prefer I beg, then beggeth I.

ORENTHAL. It's like a grotesque, never-ending dream.
What'er this game may hap to you to seem.

LANGE. Behold thyself, you've always been a man,
Endure this situation, well you can.

ORENTHAL. To be with sweet Nicole is all I wish.

LANGE. You want to see your kids, I would assume.

ORENTHAL. I've got their precious pictures here with me.

THE TRAGEDY OF ORENTHAL

LANGE. Just toss the gun outside for safety's sake,
And then no untoward action can you take.

Cowlings drives the Bronco into Orenthal estate, surrounded by many LAPD vehicles. Orenthal holds the gun to his head, sobbing.

COWLINGS. I'm begging you, don't do it, please, O.J.!

ORENTHAL. Ooooooh.

COWLINGS. I'm begging you, don't do it, hold your sway!

ORENTHAL. Aaaaaah.

COWLINGS. I pray thee, think upon the babies' heads.

Orenthal, holding framed pictures of his family, slowly emerges from the Bronco and collapses into the arms of the waiting police officers.

ORENTHAL. Now looms the next part of this waking dream!
What horrors foul from all of this shall stream?

Exeunt.

ACT IV

SCENE 1

(District attorney's office)

Enter Deputy District Attorneys Clark and Darden, Detectives Lange and Vannatter, and respective attendants.

LANGE.   I doubt that prosecution here can fail.
Of evidence a mountain we possess:
His flight from the police is where we start,
Since he who flees totes guilt upon his back;
His maudlin note of suicide admits
How far that he hath strayed from honor's path:
"Please think of the real O.J. and not this lost person."
His documented violence to Nicole;
His guilt the sisters Brown cried out at once;
An interview he barely stammered through,
In which he said "I bleedeth all the time";
Sad moans and sore laments in slow-speed chase,
Acknowledged "I'm the only one deserves"
A bullet from the pistol in his hand.
A bloody glove is found at Simpson's home,
That matches bloody glove at murder scene;
O.J.'s left hand conspicuously cut,
From which some crimson drops did likely flow.
But if these telling facts were all unknown,
The trail of blood still marks the murderer.
The blood did drip so straight to Simpson's door,

From Bundy to Bronco to Rockingham.
When science doth the DNA reveal,
It surely then the Prince's fate will seal.
Methinks Prince Juice may proffer guilty plea,
At least that's how it doth unfold to me.

CLARK.   Despite the matters you have well described
No offer of a plea has here arrived.
Not all the evidence that you recite
Will be admitted in a jury trial,
A family's burst of spite doth not convict,
Nor note that's full of ambiguity.

DARDEN.   Attorneys he doth gather left and right.
Orenthal, forsooth, prepareth for a fight:
A legal army he doth seek to wield,
Accomplices to gird him for the fray,
Some legal toughs to show him freedom's way.

VANNATTER.   His guilt I think he never will embrace,
Its consequences he could never brook,
He must seek vindication totally,
Both truth and jail he will strive to avoid.

DARDEN.   He's not hired Johnnie Cochran for a plea,
Since Cochran's game's to blame it on the cops.

CLARK.   It's true the host of lawyers he's amassed
Will cast some doubt on all the evidence.
But blood I think they cannot denigrate,
And Simpson's blood at Bundy we can place.

LANGE.   Lost soul who wrote the note of suicide,

THE TRAGEDY OF ORENTHAL

> Pathetic as he moaned in Bronco chase,
> The haggard beaten wretch I saw in court,
> Can this man stand the spotlight of a trial?
> For murder, though it have no tongue, will speak
> With most miraculous organ.[28]

DARDEN. As constable Vannatter hath observed,
Admitting guilt sits poorly in his eyes.
For one who hacks two human beings to death
No acting roles in Hollywood are left.

CLARK. The Bronco chase remains a two-edged sword.
It could produce some sympathy for him,
A poor man mourning for his love deceased,
His children lost their mother at the least.
Prepared to die, if she cannot live on,
Like Romeo, when he thought Juliet gone.

VANNATTER. The Bronco chase screams out his guilt, methinks.
It's virtually a full confessional,
Particularly when coupled with the note,
His words, to me, leave barely any doubt,
A trial must never leave these issues out.

CLARK. A host of messy choices we confront,
We best confine our case to matters clear.
A rambling presentation of all facts
Confuses, and a proper focus lacks.

DARDEN. Among the questions knocking on our door
Demanding rapid answers all too soon:
Should penalty of death be what we seek?

LANGE. To assay any less would mock the dead!
The very mercy of the law cries out
Most audible, even from his proper tongue:
Orenthal for Nicole; death for death
Haste still pays haste, and leisure answers
  leisure;
Like doth quit like, and Measure still for
  Measure.[29]

Exeunt.

SCENE 2

(Los Angeles County Jail, Orenthal's private cell)

Enter Cochran, Shapiro, and Orenthal.

COCHRAN. O.J.! What do you say? Do not dismay!
We're going to make this whole thing go away.
A brother has arrived to save the day,
No matter what CNN pundits say.

ORENTHAL. I hardly think it all will go away,
I fear there's nothing helpful I can say.

COCHRAN. The first thing we must fix is you, my Prince,
You slump around, despondent, under siege.
A man with conscience clear must stand upright,
Projecting innocence to one and all.
You wear your burden much too heavily,
And some will think it's guilt that they do see.

THE TRAGEDY OF ORENTHAL

SHAPIRO. Remember when we talk, it's privileged,
And also any talk with man of cloth.
The first thing that I think we need to know
Is how you want your plea in court to go.

ORENTHAL. The world must know a killer I am not.
For children, vindication I must seek.
I could not look into their judging eyes
And tell them that I slashed their mother's throat.

COCHRAN. Of course "not guilty" is what we'll plead.
Talk of guilt we do not need.
O.J.! Stand tall and show your pride!
The slightest hesitation you must hide.
With dignity and indignation strong,
You must walk like you're clean, strides bold and long.
But more, you must believe it in your head
Your Grace could never leave two people dead.
The Orenthal whom we all know so well
Could never see the precipice of Hell.
The outrage of one wrongfully accused,
Must also, but selectively, be used.
These thoughts with you forever must reside,
Demeanor flows from cleanliness inside.

ORENTHAL. I grasp the grisly import of your speech,
And thus for such deportment will I reach.

COCHRAN. The black man hath forever been abused,
By honky cops and troopers on the cruise,
A shakedown here, a stop and hassle there,

MICHAEL W. MONK

                Our brothers who've been beaten say beware!
                Atrocities imposed on Rodney King,
                A trial and rapt attention they did bring.
                When whitey jury freed the whitey cops,
                The riot went for days without a stop.
                Such matters must we ever keep in mind,
                Express each black man's argument we find.

SHAPIRO.   For one as eminent as thou, Prince Juice,
                A racial argument seems like abuse,
                Prince Juice a racial victim, well, he's not!
                In fact, a lavish, large estate he's got.

COCHRAN.   You miss the very heart of our defense,
                I can't imagine you could have less sense.
                Downtown L.A. is where the trial will be,
                The prosecution's choice amazes me.
                God knows why such a racial mix they chose
                Into my own backyard they stick their nose.
                I've scored my biggest victories right there
                By making all the brothers stop and stare.
                Convincing colored juries the police
                Have stumbled as they seek the Golden Fleece.
                While thoughts of Rodney King are still alive,
                Revengeful vehicle we must provide.
                If jury mainly black we can produce,
                They'll teach the world a lesson with the Juice.
                We'll scrutinize each move the cops have made
                With close inspection, they will be waylaid.
                The brothers will be quick to take the bait,
                We'll serve them racial friction on a plate.

SHAPIRO.   But theories without facts cannot proceed,

THE TRAGEDY OF ORENTHAL

                No racial evidence do I perceive,
                To push a race defense I truly fear
                Our own legal petard could hoist our rear.

ORENTHAL.   I little care what technique that we use,
                So long as my acquittal makes the news.

Exeunt.

SCENE 3
(District attorney's office)

Enter Clark, Darden, Lange, and Vannatter.

CLARK.   Like ocean swells that crash upon the shore,
                DNA washes up at Simpson's door.
                Blood at Bundy, blood at Rockingham,
                Sophisticated tests for every gram.
                And all consistent with one murderer
                Who knifed his love and took the life from her.

DARDEN.   The blood tests we've received have now
                    confirmed:
                Five drops of Simpson's blood at murder site,
                Along the path of murderer's retreat;
                His Bronco smeared with DNA of three:
                Prince Juice, Princess Nicole, and Goldman, too;
                The right-hand glove we found at Rockingham
                Hath blood of both the victims and the Juice.
                At Bundy was a matching bloody glove
                Of rarest vintage purchased by Nicole;

           The Prince's blood on Bundy's back door gate,
           That surfaced three weeks after murder night.
           A trail of blood that leads to Simpson's door.
           Bloody socks in Simpson's bedroom found,
           Not put aside, nor in the closet stored.

CLARK.   And more supporting evidence we've found:
           Rare Bruno Magli shoe prints in the blood
           Retreating once again from corpses red,
           A size 12 print, to match the Juice's foot.

VANNATTER. The DNA, I think, should act as if
           Orenthal left his business card for us;
           On five drops from the walk at Bundy scene
           We've done the most sophisticated tests:
           Both PCR and RFLP found a Simpson match
           For DNA pattern to be found
           But once in a billion human beings.
           With this conclusive scientific proof
           Provided and confirmed by DNA,
           Just frosting is all other evidence.

CLARK.   But nothing's clear when lawyers are involved,
           The simplest truth will cruelly shaded be
           With speculation wild and haughty stare.
           Just how could you perceive the sky is blue?
           They'll have you thinking you are me
           And that I might be you.
           Like bees they'll swarm around your head for
             hours.
           They'll buzz your ears with queries strange
             and new,
           Now stinging, then retreating piously.

Posturing with feigned' shock and rage,
Retracing every thought you ever had
To locate little cracks they'll label lies.
Why did you think of this? And why not
   think of that?
And do you recall such? Why can't you recall
   thus?
Can you rule out with certainty, I pray,
That Martians came to kill these innocents?

LANGE. I've scoured murder trails for many years,
And seldom had such evidence as this.

DARDEN. And the Good Lord be with us, justice, too,
Will come for this reprobate.
Till then sit still my soul. Foul deeds will rise,
Though all the earth o'erwhelm them to
   men's eyes.[30]

Exeunt.

SCENE 4
(Los Angeles County Jail, private cell of Orenthal)

Enter Rosey Grier and Orenthal.

GRIER. Kind greetings to my Prince,
How fares my brother and friend?

ORENTHAL. A joy it is for me to see your face!

GRIER.   You know that now a preacher man I am,
            Minister of the Lord for all the lambs,
            And so a talk we have is privileged
            From scrutiny by anybody else.

ORENTHAL.   I need to spill my story to a friend,
            I've kept the demons deep inside my soul.
            To beat this rap I must exude no guilt,
            So I attribute the unseemly deed
            To raging madness that's not even mine.
            But still,
            Mine eyes are made the fools o'th' other senses,
            Or else worth all the rest: I see her still;
            And on my blade, and clothes, gouts of blood
            Which was not so before.—There's no such
               thing.
            It is the bloody business which informs
            Thus to mine eyes.—Now o'er the one half-world
            Nature seems dead, and wicked dreams abuse
            The curtain'd sleep.[31]

GRIER.   Forgiveness hath no limits, I can vouch,
            For one who seeks salvation piously.

ORENTHAL.   For certain friends that are both hers and mine,
            Whose loves I may not drop, but wail her fall
            Who I myself struck down: and thence it is
            That I to your assistance do make love,
            Masking the business from the common eye,
            For sundry weighty reasons.

GRIER.   I shall, my lord
            Perform what you command.[32]

ORENTHAL. Then speak, I pray you, to my family,
Convey to them that I am innocent
And that I will steadfastly vindicate
The Simpson name that we do hold so dear.
Please let them know I need their strong support,
Please whisper soothing blessings in their ear.

GRIER. Well, heaven forgive you; and forgive us all.
Some rise by sin, and some by virtue fall.
Some run from brakes of ice and answer none,
And some condemned for a fault alone.[33]

Exeunt.

SCENE 5
(Johnnie Cochran's law offices)

Enter Cochran, Shapiro, Bailey, Scheck, and attendants.

COCHRAN. The tests for DNA do not bode well,
But whether fatal, only time will tell.
Let's hear now from genetic witch doctor,
Doth Scheck with my predictions dire concur?

SCHECK. Double, double, blood may bubble:
Proving DNA is trouble.
Scientific sorcery
Dispels the link of blood, you see,
If blood doth deteriorate,
The link we only speculate.
In DNA cauldron, cast our doubt,

MICHAEL W. MONK

                So any firm ID is out.
                Swab of goo and dab of glop
                Doth not our defense estop.
                Trainee cop and sloppy work
                Make me giggle, make me smirk.
                Since blood's so thick it's everywhere,
                Its weaknesses must come to bear.
                Indeed confusion helps our case,
                And obfuscation we'll embrace.
                For a charm of powerful trouble,
                Like a hell-broth boil and bubble.[34]

BAILEY.   But prejudice we'll also use,
                To minimize the glops and goos:
                If blood we show a cop did plant,
                Indignantly we'll rave and rant.
                If planted once we strike great fear
                That each red drop's suspicious here.

COCHRAN. Slight plausibility is all we need
                For jury to acquit its race and creed.

SHAPIRO. But planted blood! No clue of such have we!
                It seems at best invented fantasy.
                Such speculation must arise from fact,
                A grain of truth from which we can extract.

COCHRAN. Precisely so, my fellow counselor,
                Our argument must grow from seeds of fact.
                But I believe we just may have our cop,
                Bad seed on whom suspicion we can plant!
                We have investigated Fuhrman's past,
                And racist incidents are there to cast:

Of racial matters plaguing his background,
The best is a taped interview we found
In which he casually spews epithets;
With "nigger" here and "nigger" there,
He seals his bigot's fate.
Society, as you well know,
Forbids such speech of late.

BAILEY. If he admits he's talked this racist talk,
He's self-acknowledged racist on the block,
We'll chop his head off like a Christmas goose,
His head cut off, his body running loose,
If he deny that "nigger" he has spoke,
We'll shove the tape directly down his throat.

SCHECK. And furthermore, just who the hell are we
To say that Fuhrman didn't plant a glove?
If we can't say that we can rule it out
That strikes the very heart of jury doubt.
This Fuhrman says he found the second glove
At Rockingham near Kato Kaelin's house,
But at preliminary hearing here,
He spoke of observations earlier,
Describing Bundy glove, he once said "them"
Suggesting he saw two at murder scene.
If so, did he take one to Rockingham?
To nail one of the "niggers"? Yes, the Juice!
As defense, innocence we need not prove,
Just reasonable doubt! Not one bit more.
This Fuhrman fits in well with stumbling cops
And bumbling treatment of the bloody glops.

COCHRAN. And Fuhrman's just the leader of the bunch

MICHAEL W. MONK

                Conspiracy we'll show surrounds his lead.
                Coordinated planting of all blood
                Will sell to brothers in the neighborhood.
                A code of silence by the stinking cops,
                With Fuhrman others bond to frame the Prince.

SHAPIRO.   But Orenthal's the favorite of the cops,
                They let him be, protecting his bright star,
                They brushed aside his beatings of Nicole,
                Ignored domestic quarrels of the soul.
                Atrocities prophetic she endured,
                Which local cops consistently ignored.
                They're dazzled by the Juice here in L.A.
                'Twas not conspiracy to get O.J.!

COCHRAN.   That trick I've pulled a thousand times
                Don't think I can't acquittal find.
                The cops can always be abused,
                Not matter what techniques they've used.

SCHECK.   More to the point, this Fuhrman news of late
                Doth serve us up the race card on a plate.
                We have the dirt on him to make him dance
                And on the witness stand to lightly prance,
                At best he will deny the "nigger" rap
                And we will have a liar in our lap.
                Then every move he made, he falsely took,
                At least that's how that we will write the book.

                Exeunt.

THE TRAGEDY OF ORENTHAL

SCENE 6

(Orange County home of Princess Nicole's parents)

Enter Lou Brown, Juditha Brown, Denise Brown, Dominique Brown, and Detective Lange.

LANGE. I thank you for this opportunity
To interview surviving family;
Whatever thoughts you have I'd like to hear,
Perhaps to help convict the murderer.

DENISE BROWN. Know that Orenthal hath killed Nicole,
Green Monster did consume his every move.
No other man would he permit for her.
He stalked and hovered near her every step
And when they broke up weeks before she died,
Declared "I have no reason now to live."
Attraction that was fatal, literally,
That bastard took my sister's life from me.

JUDITHA BROWN. Nicole also confided fear to me.
I even heard directly from O.J.
A few months back he told me that Nicole
Was still the only woman he desired
And yet a woman that he could not have.
The month before the murder, my sweet child
Reported Simpson told her "if he ever
Saw her with another man he'd kill her."
And then one week before the bloody deed,
She told me he was following her again.
"I go to the gas station, he is there.

                    I go to Payless Shoe Store, he is there.
                    I'm driving, he is in my rearview mirror."

DENISE   I, too, heard threats he made two weeks before
BROWN.   He slaughtered our Nicole.

JUDITHA   But nothing that we say brings back our girl.
BROWN.   My daughter's gory death befouls my dreams.
                   To see your child deceased while you live on
                   Doth kill part of a parent's living heart.
                   And worse, this horror plagueth not just me:
                   Two cherubs heavenly are now bereft
                   Of loving mother's tender, soft caress.

DENISE   And yet his lawyers plot for his defense
BROWN.   With press conference and sinful posturing.
                   I wonder if his deed they comprehend,
                   Think'st they of knife thrust into human flesh
                   Or of the defiled corpses left behind?
                   To them it's just a game to set him free,
                   Without a thought about the tragedy.

LOU BROWN.   But oh, how vile an idol proves this God!
                   Thou hath, Orenthal, done good feature
                     shame.
                   In nature, there's no blemish but the mind;
                   None can be called deformed but the unkind.
                   Virtue is beauty; but the beauteous evil
                   Are empty trunks o'er-flourished by the devil.[35]

Exeunt.

THE TRAGEDY OF ORENTHAL

SCENE 7

(Judge Ito's courtroom, Los Angeles County Superior Court, Wednesday, September 27, 1995)

Enter Judge Ito, jury, defendant Orenthal, Cochran, Shapiro, Scheck, Clark and Darden, Court Personnel, attendants, and observers to a flourish of trumpets.

JUDGE ITO. Dear jury, we for many months have heard
From witnesses profound, and some absurd,
And for the last two days the argument
Presented by counselors from the State.
How now? It seems we're ready to proceed
With closing argument from the defense.
So Mr. Cochran, you may now begin.

COCHRAN. For Orenthal James Simpson I'll now speak:
A man completely mild and kind and meek.
You've heard all the evidence
Day by day and mile by mile,
You probably wonder, like I do:
Why we even havin' a trial?
Orenthal's innocent, I think that's clear!
And so I say, case closed, why are we here?
But I'm not here to argue this with you,
Just reasonable inferences I'll spew.
A jury truly marvelous you've been,
The most patient and healthy one I've seen.
The longest serving jury in L.A.
You have a chance to make the black man's day.
Heed not the words in Darden's sermon.
Instead the facts are yours to determine.

MICHAEL W. MONK

Fair Sister Rose hath said some time ago
That "he who violates his oath profanes
Divinity of sacred faith himself,"
And Abraham Lincoln, who did express
That jury service is the highest act
Of citizenship for our country dear.
I have no doubt a jury bright as this
My client's innocence will ever miss.
But just remember 'midst all of this strife,
We're fighting for the Prince's very life.
You are empowered to do justice here
Each one of you can rectify a smear.
Frederick Douglass, a favorite of mine,
One hundred years ago did so opine:
"No rich, no poor, no high, no low
No white, no black in this country
But equal rights, in all the fights,
A truly common destiny."
This goal we've not yet reached, so says our race.
But you can help our nation in this case:
True justice in America,
Your verdict will bespeak.
Are the police above the law
No matter what they wreak?
The evidence doth clearly show
Police conspiracy did grow.
A foul agenda had the cops:
The Prince alone they sought to stop.
And untrained officers did bungle,
Traipsing through the bloody jungle.
Routine procedures they delayed,
Through vanity, mistakes they made.
The evidence, so bold and gory,

Is inconsistent with their story.
At 10:40 the dogs first bark.
Yet at 10:40 thumps they mark
On Kato Kaelin's bungalow
As Simpson hit the wall just so.
They'd have you think at 10:40
In two places the Juice could be.
Next on Vannatter let's expound:
He carried Simpson's blood around;
Who knows just where the blood he smeared?
Blood has been found in spots absurd.
We proved to you the glove won't fit.
If it doesn't fit, you must acquit.

JUDGE ITO. If fitting time this be to interrupt,
In recess we will stand for thirty minutes.
Our jurors' minds can use a little space,
Before more exhortations on the case.

Court recesses for 30 minutes.

JUDGE ITO. Counselor Cochran, continuest thou may.

COCHRAN. Ms. Clark did state in argument
Mountains of evidence they've lent
And oceans, too, of evidence,
But none of it makes any sense.
Lo! Mountains now like molehills seem,
The ocean shrinks to a tiny stream.
They talk about a trail of blood
This argument's a total dud:
Glove which they found at Juice compound
Was on a patch of virgin ground

MICHAEL W. MONK

And in the space that did surround,
No other bloody drops were found.
On this I will not rave or rant,
But just suggest a clear-cut plant.
How was the second glove produced?
Our local bigot on the loose!
Perjurer and racist foul,
He planted glove on solo prowl.
Think about Prince Juice's house
We took you there to look about.
No blood on doorknob you did see
No blood on light switch seen by me,
No blood on banister to spy
A pristine carpet met your eye.
Do you believe that Simpson bleedeth
Just when prosecution needeth?
And just what of the cap of knit,
No real disguise provideth it,
It makes no sense, it doesn't fit.
If it doesn't fit, you must acquit.
Just like the glove experiment
In mind a vision doth imprint,
For scores of years you'll not forget
The bloody glove just didn't fit.
They've wrongfully accused the Juice
Pure innocence deserves no noose.
A rush to judgment we have seen,
No search for truth was there to glean.
Cynical and speculative,
No solid proof have they to give.
If you have any reasonable doubt,
You've got to throw the charges out.
As jury you must use the facts,

THE TRAGEDY OF ORENTHAL

Not let emotion rule thy acts.
And so these thoughts I now present.
To jury most intelligent.
Clark points to family argument
In which we heard hard feelings spent.
If murder's proved by family spat
In jail is where we'd all be at!
Then Cyndy Garvey testified
A brooding, angry Juice she spied.
But no! On party video
Just waves and smiles he doth bestow.
When stories and tall tales arrive
A video dispels the jive.
You know it, I know it, we all know it!
Just look now at this human being,
Prince Orenthal is who I mean,
Who, wrongfully accused, has sat
With dignity still all intact.
Especially Vannatter's lie
That Juice was no suspected guy.
So anyone who now believes
Police are perfect, misconceives.
Those who think police don't lie,
And all cop prejudice doth die,
And those who discount racism
Respond with flippant sarcasm,
They do live in a world of dreams,
And miss realities obscene.
Simpson, Simpson! He's our man!
If he can't be acquitted, what black man can?

JUDGE ITO.   I think we will conclude our session now
And jury, I again admonish you:

	The facts you can't amongst yourselves discuss Or form opinions now upon the case. Tomorrow Mr. Cochran will conclude His argument. But now we do recess.
ORENTHAL.	*[Aside.]* My heart prepares to fly with freedom's hope. I sense the battle here can now be won. Perhaps no sordid prison cell awaits, If jury feels the power of our plea. Yet people are at times so hard to read, And jurors seem to pose emotionless, Masked in a poker game of life or death. One moment I am sure we will hold sway, But next, the bloody truth seems obvious. And then I will, indignant, fume away At Fuhrman and the bigotry he wrought. Is not this case the proper one to purge The outrages of centuries unjust? But single-minded thirst for my release Doth dominate my thoughts above all else. Even a haunted freedom, fraught with doubt, Would be the sweetest water I could drink. I'll later make my peace within my heart, Acquittal from this crime must be the start.
	Cochran, Scheck, and Shapiro join Orenthal in a conference room.
SCHECK.	This lengthy game is finally near the end; Sir Cochran doth a stirring sermon lend. I think our sorcery of DNA doth cloud The value of contaminated blood.

THE TRAGEDY OF ORENTHAL

ORENTHAL.   My hopes are tempered with uncertainty.

COCHRAN.   Thou must a noble gentleman remain,
And stride with dignity and self-respect.
Just walk with head erect and hiding naught,
Indignant at thy fate, but confident:
An innocent man wrongfully accused.
A trial is but a play that we produce,
And each of us play well our given role.
While true your part is not a speaking one,
Because the Fifth Amendment hath been used,
Your carriage, your demeanor, attitude,
The scent of innocence you must exude.
When on the morrow I conclude your case,
Our play must perfect be in courtroom space.

Exeunt.

SCENE 8
(Judge Ito's courtroom, Los Angeles County Superior Court, Thursday, September 28, 1995)

Enter Orenthal, Judge Ito, jury, Cochran, lawyers, witnesses, and spectators to a flourish of trumpets.

JUDGE ITO.   Good morning, ladies and fine gentlemen,
With Mr. Cochran we again begin.

COCHRAN.   Just yesterday we covered many things
That I will now proceed to summarize:
This trial is all about a racist cop.

Mark Fuhrman's at the core of why we're here.
A lying genocidal racist he,
Who in a letter written did admit
"Each interracial couple I will stop
And I'll create a reason if I must."
You saw him lie upon the witness stand
Said "n" word he'd not said in ten full years,
And then the horrid racist tapes we heard
In which Mark Fuhrman used the "nigger" word.
He lied about his meeting Kathy Bell!
He lied about the "nigger" word he said!
This is the very man who on his own
Coincidentally found the bloody glove.
And so we see the messengers we have
Are reprehensible in every way.
Twin demons of deception are these two!
Mark Fuhrman and Vannatter and their lies,
They bring a message that we cannot trust.
Vannatter's big lies! Fuhrman's big lies!
Vannatter, the man who carried the blood,
Fuhrman, the man who found the glove.
If Fuhrman saw at Bundy just one glove,
Why did he speak of "them" instead of "it"?
Mark Fuhrman, even Marcia Clark admits,
He is America's worst nightmare cop.
Twin demons of evil have we here.
So jury, now, this nightmare you must stop!
If you don't stop this cover-up, who will?
Do you think the police are going to stop?
Do you think the DA is going to stop?
Think you that we can stop it by ourselves?

THE TRAGEDY OF ORENTHAL

It has to be stopped by you!
Who polices the police?
You police the police!
Twin demons of evil:
Vannatter and Fuhrman.
From Hades comes this Fuhrman devil foul!
This Lucifer whom you have heard express
That all the niggers he would like to see
Gathered together, and then burned or
  bombed.
So shaken I, his words I can't recall,
But just that Fuhrman said he'd kill them all.
Like genocide that Adolf Hitler wrought,
Because the world his killings did not stop.
Mark Fuhrman you have heard express his hate:
"The only good nigger is a dead nigger."
Twin devils of deception you can't trust!
Vannatter says they're not here to save lives
Yet later claims that it was just a joke!
If you can't trust the messenger, you see,
The message hath no credibility.
But let me leave you with a single thought,
About equality we all have sought:
As great as is America to me,
We've not yet reached racial equality.
But you and I can fight for freedom now!
Such bigotry our country can't allow!
And genocidal racists we'll expose
Wherever that we find injustice goes.
If you don't speak out!
If you don't stand up!
If you don't do what's right!
Equality we never will achieve.

MICHAEL W. MONK

Life, liberty, and justice just a dream!
You've evidence by which you can acquit,
Black dignity your verdict must befit.
Simpson, Simpson!
He's our man!
If he can't be acquitted,
What black man can?
Simpson, Simpson!
He's our man!
If he can't be acquitted,
What black man can?

Exeunt.

ACT V

SCENE 1
(LAPD offices of Lange and Vannatter)

Enter Lange and Vannatter.

VANNATTER. How dare he label me a Fuhrman twin?
A lifelong honest cop is what I've been,
Now painted Devil and conspirator.
A simple oversight, I carried blood,
Blood drawn from vessels of a murderer;
But plant the blood? No way I could or would!
Mark Fuhrman did not find a second glove,
Since sixteen cops came first to murder scene,
Each one of whom did scour the place with care.
But even if one disregards the gloves,
The damning blood found everywhere should make
The jury pierce right through John Cochran's rant,
His puffing, posturing and bullying.

LANGE. A lawyer most adroit, a slimy man,
He brings new outrage to the "shyster" world,
Reveling in confusion he creates.

VANNATTER. I almost more do blame the judge himself,
Who let defense pure garbage long explore,
Perhaps his 15 minutes to prolong.
Manipulated, weak, and variable,
He lost control quite early in the game.

MICHAEL W. MONK

LANGE. And all the facts our lawyers didn't use!
A host of stories that they failed to tell,
That seemed to me to make the matter clear.
They're not like you and I, methodical
In every word we speak and thought we have.
When Fuhrman colored every policeman's step,
Our lawyers sought some distance from the cops.
We saw persuasive evidence not used;
The jury heard none of the following:
For one, Nicole's taped voice expressing fear;
Second, Simpson's knife-killing fantasy
Confirmed by Eastern limo driving man;
Third, Dominique Brown's flawless shoe ID
Regarding Bruno Magli shoes Juice wore;
Fourth, witness who saw Simpson dump a bag
In airport trash can on the murder eve;
Then zipped he up his travel bag posthaste;
Fifth, Chicago Hertz rep who puzzled at
"How empty" Simpson's travel bag did seem;
Sixth, the interview we held and taped
In which no remote alibi he had;
Seventh, the note of suicide ignored,
Though Prince Juice as a guilty man implored;
Eighth, too, the Bronco chase when Simpson fled;
Ninth, the conversation 'midst the chase;
Tenth, the telling gear Simpson procured:
Wig, money, gun, and passport for his use;
Eleventh are the keys to Nicole's house
They found in one of Simpson's travel bags.
While anyone a trial can second-guess,
We left out evidence that was our best.

VANNATTER.   To simplify this case hath proved a bitch,
             Some of the evidence they had to pitch.
             But items ten plus one of which you speak
             Seem crucial for the verdict that we seek.
             But all is one if my suspicion's true.
             I must believe the blood will get us through.

LANGE.   I'm haunted by the firmly held belief
             This jury will give justice no relief.
             Prince Orenthal the jury will acquit
             Within two days at Rockingham he'll sit.

             Exeunt.

SCENE 2
(District attorney's office)

Enter Clark and Darden.

CLARK.   Gargantuan debacle we have seen!
             This trial has now careened out of control.
             The judge admitted speculation raw
             And fishing expeditions vast and bold.
             No evidence of drug deals has been shown,
             Yet questions as to such have rampant been.
             Inquiries most extraneous we've seen
             Regarding Fuhrman statements long ago.
             The cops have been impeached and vilified.
             One cop emergeth racist reprobate,
             Another carries Simpson's blood about
             As if it were the morning newspaper

	And not the very proof of Simpson's guilt.
DARDEN.	I fear that Cochran's simple legal tack Will have the jury disregard the cuts That sent two souls to heaven on that night. But notwithstanding circus atmosphere, Still undisputed evidence we have That should return a verdict full of guilt. A murderer's a murderer, my friend, Whatever be the color of his skin.
CLARK.	Of jurors twelve, nine blacks will cast a vote. A surly, sour bunch they do appear, In part because they have sequestered been, Ensconced in hotel suites as prisoners. And if my sense of people not deceive Strong racial anger, too, I do perceive. They'd like to relegate the cops to hell. For Fuhrman's bigotry they did hear tell. Lord Cochran plays them like a violin, Exacerbating tensions with his spin. 'Tis not the Prince's guilt that they will see, But just a chance for racial victory.
DARDEN.	But how can Cochran with complete straight face Contend Vannatter's out to soil my race? Vannatter clearly no agenda had To smear him so seems eminently sad.
CLARK.	But can this jury really set him free When honest minds perceive he is guilty? We must not make a scarecrow of the law,

Setting it up to fear the birds of prey,
And let it keep one shape till custom make it
Their perch, and not their terror.[36]

Exeunt.

SCENE 3
(Judge Ito's courtroom, Los Angeles County Superior Court)

*Enter Judge Ito, Orenthal, lawyers, attendants,
court personnel, and spectators.*

JUDGE ITO. The jury hath deliberations done,
And now return with verdict form complete.
Madame Clerk, please read aloud their say.

COURT
CLERK.
In the matter of the People of California
Versus Orenthal James Simpson,
We the jury find the defendant Not Guilty
Of the murder of Nicole Brown Simpson.
We the jury find the defendant Not Guilty
Of the murder of Ronald Lyle Goldman.

ORENTHAL. Thank you for my life and freedom's sake!
No more benign decision could you make!
A brave new world now opens up to me,
Broad vistas, blue horizons I can see!

JUDGE ITO. The jury now hath spoken, I decree,
Prince Orenthal is now completely free.

Jury stands and files out with one juror thrusting a clenched fist into the air, and reporters now proceed to interview the jury.

Enter Reporters.

REPORTER. Less than one day thou didst deliberate.
Why didst thou judge that freedom is his fate?

JUROR ONE. For months we've muted sat and captive been,
Sequestered and secluded from our lives.

JUROR TWO. The racist and the bungling cops we've seen:
Vile Fuhrman would exterminate our race.
Our fate was to negate such bigotry.

JUROR THREE. The bond with police has long ago been cleft;
Our worst suspicions all have been confirmed.

JUROR FOUR. 'Tis possible that O.J. did the deed,
But it has not been proven to our taste.

JUROR FIVE. Our buds do sense a reasonable doubt
The prosecution did not make its case.

JUROR SIX. It's time the black man had some court support!
I know Mark Fuhrman planted O.J.'s glove.
That serpent would do almost anything.

JUROR SEVEN. I have my doubts about DNA hype,
Since lots of people have the same blood type.

THE TRAGEDY OF ORENTHAL

JUROR   The evil work of racists like this cop
EIGHT.   Do plague us more than any murder can.

JUROR   Brothers are murdered every single day,
NINE.   For these poor souls I see no cop doth pray.

JUROR TEN.   The wretched and the poor are human, too,
                Even if such Africans we be.

JUROR   We're not street animals to be destroyed,
ELEVEN.   For all, equal respect must be employed.

JUROR   Simpson, Simpson,
TWELVE.   He's our man!
                If he can't be acquitted,
                What black man can!
                Simpson, Simpson!
                He's our man!
                If he can't be acquitted,
                What black man can?

ALL JURORS.   Simpson, Simpson!
                He's our man!
                If he can't be acquitted,
                What black man can?
                Black man can!
                Black man can!
                Black man can!
                Black man can!

                Exeunt.

SCENE 4
(Prince Orenthal's Rockingham estate)

Enter Orenthal, Prince's mother, Arnelle, Jason, other Simpson family members, Cowlings, Kardashian, Lords Cochran and Shapiro, and various guests and attendants for party to celebrate Simpson's acquittal.

PRINCE'S MOTHER. Come to me now, my child, and give a hug.
Come let me give you Mother's tender kiss,
To think that my sweet child now can be free.
My darkest fears can now be buried deep.

ORENTHAL. *[Aside.]*
I fear that just Nicole is buried deep.
This thought, like others, I will private keep.

[To Mother.]
I thank the Lord for our good fortune,
Mom; we now can start to piece together lives,
Not just for me but all our family.
We have been tested long and rigorously.

COWLINGS. How is the sweetest mom of all I know?
Give me a hug for your huge victory.
O.J., this is your greatest win of all,
Eclipsing the most famous of the past!
No football game compares to life in jail,
Thank God you have survived this great travail!

ORENTHAL. I hope the nightmare now can start to end,
Of that I can assure you, my sweet friend.
My deepest inner fears and monsters gross

THE TRAGEDY OF ORENTHAL

                Have been dissected before all the world,
                Seamy soap opera for daytime TV,
                These matters have forever tainted me.

KARDASHIAN.   Sweet greetings, Prince, please let me shake thy hand,
                I've bursting been with happiness for thee!

ORENTHAL.   Give me a hug, and let me say to thee,
                A friend most steadfast thou hast proved to be.
                Thank you for all and more that you have done!
                We've finally beaten back the grisly beast
                Of criminal proceedings and their grief.
                Please make my home your home for all your days.

SHAPIRO.   Greetings to thee, my Prince, now freedom's man.
                I'm truly glad that liberation's yours.
                I humbly wish you now the precious gift
                To stride ahead and let the foul fog lift.

KARDASHIAN.   O.J.! Come say hello to a juror,
                Who's come to pay respects to you and yours
                For freedom we will party till we drop!
                No jail will now Prince Juice's movement stop.

JUROR.   Sweet Prince, you are so very kind to me,
                To let me join with such celebrities,
                I'm proud of what our jury members did
                To make our brother proud, and strong, and free.

ORENTHAL.   I am to you indebted,
For what you did for me.
I'm pleased to have you here,
For my hospitality.

COCHRAN.   Say hey! Big guy! No longer be aware,
I smell the balm of freedom in the air.
Thy heart must dance like that of birthday child!
No longer are thy garments prison-styled!

ORENTHAL.   Somewhat in shock is what I seem to be.
Waves of relief still wash across my soul,
All at once I'm cleansed, and I am free.
Visions I see of pleasant restaurants
And rolling fairways leading to a green.
To come and go each moment as I please
Looms as a life that's full of grace and ease.
Yet still there's something large that gnaws at me:
My soul's still uncertain destiny.

COCHRAN.   When prison bar doth suddenly swing free
Imprisoned still the prisoner may be,
As lion back and forth will boldly pace
Despite an open zoo door in its face.
You'll soon regain a taste for freedom's fruit,
That's clear to all, no matter how astute.

Exeunt.

THE TRAGEDY OF ORENTHAL

SCENE 5
(Brentwood Country Club)

Enter Felix, Parm, and Storm in the middle of a round of golf.

FELIX. Two hours to deliberate the case,
One hundred twenty minutes of their life,
And on the heels of months of evidence,
Of testimony detailed and complex.
Most quickly their agenda they pursued.

PARM. While Simpson did kill two, it little meant:
Strong racial tension Cochran did foment.
Inside my heart an anger now doth swell,
That guilt so palpable is brushed aside.
To free a murderer serves no one's case,
Since punishment cannot depend on race.
Do each of us retreat into our kind,
And make Fair Justice blush with silent shame?
John Cochran is despicable and vile,
First matter, he doth incite racial hate
And thereby he doth loose a murderer.
Next there he is, on camera smilingly,
Obsequiously preaching harmony,
Among the races in society,
As if he were not all too recently
Inflaming blacks at every white that be.
A haunting tape just last night I did see:
At Indiana University,
When verdict was announced on the TV,
The students watching in the law school lounge,
Like separate warring factions, did respond:

The students black did yelp with joy and glee,
And nary an exception I did see,
While each Caucasian student I observed
With gloomy countenance did sit in shock.
Should not law students merely weigh the facts,
And make a reasoned judgment on the case?
With some of each race different in their view,
Instead of seeking to defend a hue?
Good Dr. King taught color not to judge
But look instead at human character.
But also now a hero I have lost,
Since I revered the Prince like all the rest.
Some small bit of respect perhaps I'd have,
If Orenthal admitted what he'd done,
But prostitute he is and killer foul,
I hope he aches each moment of each day.

STORM.   I think you take it all too personally.
Perhaps it's just a single man released,
A man who recently we much admired.
You wouldn't admit guilt if it were you,
We'd all do what we could for "not guilty."
And if it took a sordid racial plea,
With passion I would sing it to get free.
Maybe a win for blacks can purpose serve,
And help to let the tension all subside,
Like lancing a most puffing painful boil,
Releasing all the pressure brings relief,
Despite the pain the process doth entail.

PARM.   I had no doubt he killed her from the start,
'Twas personal and came straight from the
   heart,

No hit of drug professional was this,
Rather, spurned lover's never-ending wrath.
But saddest is the ethnic legacy,
Blacks lost an honored member of their race
Who first bridged many racial barriers,
But now Prince Juice forever is disgraced.
My mind doth drift back to the '60s time,
When we'd become a single family,
Brothers and sisters of all races and colors
Singing Sly Stone's Woodstock harmony.
But now each race doth different seek to be,
Attempts to be unique for all to see,
And worse we now want others us to pay
For each little burden we think we bear.
The last thing that we want is equality,
Since that would lack a preference for me.

FELIX.　　　The issue's not so simple, I must say,
Since bigotry remains unto this day,
And preference, if used judiciously,
Can open doors at times deservedly.
But these events have set us back indeed,
When rich white women march so silently
Through the streets of Santa Monica,
And Brentwood's San Vicente Boulevard,
With candles on a vigil for Nicole.
Such demonstrations show an anger deep,
Which plague us all, whatever view we keep.

Exeunt.

SCENE 6
(Brentwood restaurant)

*Enter Orenthal, Cowlings, and attendants; Maître d',
patrons, and staff.*

ORENTHAL. Good eve to thee, fair local Maître d',
The corner booth we have reserved for six.
A pleasure to this eatery explore,
For each of us proceeding through the door.
For purposes of privacy, I beg
Please give us leave to enter quietly.

MAÎTRE D'. The reservation for the Cowlings group?
I do recall the name is on the list;
Please wait a moment in the bar, I beg,
I'll check to see that all is now prepared.

COWLINGS. The table's set, I see it as we speak,
Please let us through so we can take our seat.

MAÎTRE D'. I beg your pardon, sir, I do require
Your patience, if I may a moment have.

ORENTHAL. What is this haughty greeting that we get?
Such rudeness I would hope we had not met.
He clearly recognizes I am me;
His shoulder holds a chip, most obviously.

MAÎTRE D'. Please follow me, your table is prepared.

*Orenthal and Cowlings party are seated at a corner
table.*

THE TRAGEDY OF ORENTHAL

PATRON ONE. Mine eyes observe a serpent, I believe;
A lying scummy murderer is here.
Cowlings and Orenthal disgrace our space!
How dare they show their face in public place?

PATRON TWO. Prince Orenthal's not welcome in my sight,
His sordid presence I won't lightly take.
He may have conned a racist jury pool,
But no one here in Brentwood does he fool.
A bloody murderer is what he is!
Two innocents are buried in the ground
While like celebrity he struts around.
I now shall seek his ouster or depart.
Waiter! I must see the Maître d' at once!
We have a grave emergency!

MAÎTRE D'. Good sir, I'm here to please you if I may.
What service can I now provide for thee?

PATRON TWO. With murderers I do not choose to mix,
Yet murderer I smell at this repast!
A loyal patron of this restaurant,
I must demand that this "Prince" leave at once,
If he doth not, my group will soon depart,
Never to return, please mark my heart.
He slit two throats as all the world doth know.
Please order him to leave, or else I go.

MAÎTRE D'. I understand your sensitivity,
But can we not proceed without dispute?

PATRON ONE. That is exactly what we cannot do!
He leaveth now or you will have revolt;

I see the other customers do fret,
His presence will befoul each bite we eat.
The atmosphere already grows most tense.
I'll soon shout what my view of butchers be
If he is not removed quite hastily.

Maître d'. Precipitous there is no need to be.
I will explore this matter with the Prince.

Maître d' approaches Orenthal's table.

Good my lord, one brief moment I beseech,
I have a grave concern to share with you.

Orenthal. Well, my concern is your intrusion rude.

Maître d'. No, sir, I am most deadly serious.

Orenthal. I say, sir, dost thou mock me with thy words?
What talkest thee of "grave" and "deadly" here?

Maître d'. I seekest not to open painful wounds,
But I do have a customer revolt.
Our restaurant most chilly hath become,
Perhaps it's best that we avoid a scene.

Orenthal. A scene you seem determined to provoke!

Maître d'. Publicity unkind will kill us here.
Let's steer away from such adversity.

Orenthal. Thou must be either idiot or cad,
But surely quite enough of this I've had.

THE TRAGEDY OF ORENTHAL

COWLINGS.   Such impudence we will not tolerate,
            Come, let's away to a more gracious state.

ORENTHAL.   Revengeful and small-minded do they seem.
            Such fools are best avoided if one can.
            I'll rise above all bigotry like this,
            No matter what they all do think of me.

COWLINGS.   Let's head to Rockingham and order in,
            No need to fight such gross intolerance.
            We'll take our meal out of the public light.

            *Exeunt all but Orenthal, who slowly walks to
            his car.*

ORENTHAL.   The days of adulation are far gone,
            A distant bitter memory for me.
            Instead of fighting off the autographs,
            I now must slink in unobtrusively,
            Lest some indignant bitch for women's rights
            Doth shout straight in my face too stridently.
            It's battered this, and battered that, for them,
            No sense of all the feces I did taste.
            The jury did acquit me in the show,
            They speculate about what they don't know.
            I still have some support within my race,
            In such support my faith I now must place.
            Close friends mean more than fickle fame to me:
            One is a rock, the other fantasy.

            Exit.

MICHAEL W. MONK

SCENE 7
(Rancho Park Municipal Golf Course)

Enter Orenthal, with golf bag, seeking a foursome.

ORENTHAL. How long ago my life before her death,
A magic time I barely can recall,
A foggy broken dream of luxury
So real but now evaporated, gone!
A movie star, commercials by the score,
Superstar for rent-a-car was I,
And Foster Grants to shade my famous eyes.
A football commentator nationally,
A mansion full of bounty and excess,
More income sources than I can recall.
Most of all, beloved by all the land,
A hero in each room where I did stand.
A golden bride whom I did love so true,
The mother of my precious girl and boy.
But now look at the viper I've become:
My golf club, Riviera, tossed me out.
On public courses I must prowl about.
I'm forced to beg for strangers I can join,
The foursomes are not always there for me;
An interloper in a stranger's group,
Instead of Hertz's guest whom all adore.
The glory of "not guilty" faded fast,
The civil jury found me liable,
Investigators track each dime I make.
My pension is alone untouchable;
And all that doth remain for me today,
Yet my expenses, it must fully pay.
No acting or endorsements will I see,

No contract to announce a football game.
They've taken Rockingham away from me,
The owner new did knock it to the ground.
No physical reminder of the days
Of wine and roses in a golden haze.
E'en my Heisman Trophy has been seized
And sold at auction as a ghoulish toy;
Football jerseys autographed were bought
And burned as public protest of my acts.
The summer of my life is clearly gone,
Its balmy sunshine now hath long since passed;
Autumn winds now bring a chilly day
And winter's icy fangs I soon will see,
Somber in themselves, in any case,
But much more painful due to summer's loss,
And I a summer had like few will see.
'Twould all be different now, were she alive,
But forces past my scope controlled that day.
A role that I seemed destined to portray,
She fouled the whole thing up for both of us.
She could have left me with a touch of pride,
But she, revengeful, flaunted dalliance,
Embarrassed me in open public view.
She knew I would not tolerate her act,
And with the devil she did make a pact.
But by my troth, naught's had, all's spent,
Where our desire is got without content:
'Tis safer to be that which we destroy,
Than by destruction dwell in doubtful joy.[37]
Most grisly though of all the infamy
Is how I fear my children look at me.
How often do they think upon their mom
And wonder if my hands did slice her throat?

While they must know I love them with my life,
Within each hug, I feel their painful strife.

Enter a threesome of golfers approaching the first tee.

ORENTHAL. How now! Good my lords, most humbly I beseech,
Could you a fourth use for this morning's round?
Prince Orenthal's my name, and here's my hand,
I'll gladly join your merry little band.

GOLFER. With all respect that's due to you, good Prince,
Methinks that we would simply rather not.
We'll not impede your all-consuming search,
Your quest to find the real murderer.
We humbly bid adieu to you, good sir.

Exeunt all but Prince Orenthal, standing with his golf bags.

NOTES

[References are to *The Arden Shakespeare Complete Works*, Third Series, 1998]

ACT I

1. p. 7—The Prologue is drawn nearly verbatim from *Hamlet*, Act V, Scene II, lines 384–393.

2. p. 11—The preceding four lines are taken verbatim from *Romeo and Juliet*, Act I, Scene V, lines 44–47.

3. p. 20—The preceding four lines are taken verbatim from *The Two Gentlemen of Verona*, Act II, Scene IV, lines 211–214.

4. p. 24—The preceding eight lines are taken verbatim from *Macbeth*, Act II, Scene III, lines 54–61.

5. p. 25—The preceding two lines are taken verbatim from *Macbeth*, Act II, Scene IV, lines 5–6.

6. p. 25—The preceding seven lines are taken verbatim from *Henry IV*, Part I, Act III, Scene I, lines 24–30.

7. p. 29—The preceding seven lines are drawn nearly verbatim from *Macbeth*, Act I, Scene V, lines 61–67.

ACT II

8. p. 34—The preceding eleven lines are taken verbatim from *Othello*, Act III, Scene III, lines 271–281.

9. p. 36—The preceding two lines are taken verbatim from *Macbeth*, Act III, Scene I, lines 26–27.

10. p. 37—The preceding four lines are drawn nearly verbatim from *Macbeth*, Act IV, Scene I, lines 83–86.

11. p. 37—The preceding six lines are taken verbatim from *Macbeth*, Act I, Scene III, lines 137–142.

12. p. 37—The preceding four lines are taken verbatim from *Macbeth*, Act I, Scene IV, lines 50–53.

13. p. 38—The preceding five lines are taken verbatim from *Macbeth*, Act I, Scene V, lines 49–53.

14. p. 38—The preceding four lines are taken verbatim from *Macbeth*, Act IV, Scene I, lines 44–47.

15. p. 39—The preceding nine lines are taken verbatim from *Othello*, Act V, Scene II, lines 77–85.

16. p. 39—The preceding four lines are drawn in part from *Hamlet*, Act I, Scene I, lines 1–3.

17. p. 41—The preceding two lines are drawn nearly verbatim from *Macbeth*, Act III, Scene I, lines 140–141.

18. p. 44—The preceding two lines are drawn in part from *Macbeth*, Act I, Scene III, lines 148–149.

19. p. 45—The preceding four lines are taken verbatim from *Macbeth*, Act II, Scene II, lines 59–62.

THE TRAGEDY OF ORENTHAL

20. p. 47—The preceding two lines are taken verbatim from *Macbeth*, Act I, Scene VII, lines 82–83.

21. p. 48—The preceding fifteen lines are drawn in part from *Measure for Measure*, Act IV, Scene IV, lines 21–35.

22. p. 49—The preceding four lines are drawn loosely from *Macbeth*, Act V, Scene I, lines 27–41.

ACT III

23. p. 79—The preceding two lines are taken verbatim from *Henry V*, Act II, Scene IV, lines 145–146.

24. p. 80—The preceding four lines are taken verbatim from *Macbeth*, Act I, Scene VII, lines 9–12.

25. p. 84—The preceding fifteen lines are drawn mostly verbatim from *Hamlet*, Act V, Scene II, lines 228–243.

26. p. 85—The preceding six lines are drawn nearly verbatim from *Macbeth*, Act II, Scene III, lines 89–94.

27. p. 85—The preceding seven lines are drawn nearly verbatim from *Macbeth*, Act III, Scene II, lines 17–23.

ACT IV

28. p. 93—The preceding two lines are taken verbatim from *Hamlet*, Act II, Scene II, lines 595–596.

29. p. 94—The preceding five lines are drawn nearly verbatim from *Measure for Measure*, Act V, Scene I, lines 404–408.

30. p. 99—The preceding two lines are taken verbatim from *Hamlet*, Act I, Scene II, lines 257–258.

31. p. 100—The preceding eight lines are drawn in large part from *Macbeth*, Act II, Scene I, lines 44–51.

32. p. 100—The preceding eight lines are drawn in large part from *Macbeth*, Act III, Scene I, lines 120–127.

33. p. 101—The preceding four lines are drawn nearly verbatim from *Measure for Measure*, Act II, Scene I, lines 37–40.

34. p. 102—The preceding eighteen lines are very loosely based upon *Macbeth*, Act IV, Scene I, lines 10–19.

35. p. 106—The preceding six lines are drawn nearly verbatim from *Twelfth Night*, Act III, Scene IV, lines 364–369.

ACT V

36. p. 121—The preceding four lines are taken verbatim from *Measure for Measure*, Act II, Scene I, lines 1–4.

37. p. 135—The preceding four lines are drawn nearly verbatim from *Macbeth*, Act III, Scene II, lines 4–7.

CPSIA information can be obtained at www.ICGtesting.com
Printed in the USA
BVOW03*0101150414

350129BV00001B/3/P

9 781937 650360